october FOREVER

Katie Cawood

For all the spooky people who start decorating
for Halloween on September 1st

Author's Note

Welcome to Underwood, Michigan!

October Forever was never part of my plan, but here we are. I'm a big Halloween girlie, and sometime in July, I challenged myself to write a Halloween "novella" before October. I thought this would end up being a 100-page story, but Lucy and Cameron demanded more. Having said that, it's still a relatively quick read you can probably finish in one weekend. Highly recommend curling up with your favorite blanket and a cup of something hot while you read!

A gentle warning: while this story is cozy and heartfelt, it also contains a few detailed sex scenes.

Lastly, two characters from the Woodvale series might pop up in this book. But they're not named, so let's see if you can spot them!

-Katie

Playlist

"There She Goes" - The La's
"Mystery of Love" - Sufjan Stevens
"Autumn Town Leaves" - Iron & Wine
"House of My Soul" - Langhorne Slim
"welcome and goodbye" - Dream, Ivory
"Always Forever" - Cult
"Automne" – Alexandra Streliski
"Season of the Witch" - Lana Del Rey
"Stand By Me" - Florence + the Machine
"If We Were Vampires" - Jason Isbell & the 400 Unit
"Please, Please, Please, Let Me Get What I Want" - The Smiths

Chapter One

Lucy

"Please don't make me deal with her."

I clutched my clipboard to my chest, glancing from my mom to my dad with pleading eyes—the same way I did when I begged them to let me keep the Shetland pony we rented for my tenth birthday party. And, just like then, they were completely unmoved.

"She's the daughter of a state senator," my mom said, smoothing a non-existent wrinkle from her silk blouse, the picture of calm. But of course she was calm. Now that I was back, she treated me like her personal assistant, assigning me every task she didn't want to bother with. "This is one bride we don't want to tick off, Lucy."

My parents and I stood off to the side of the lobby of The Underwood Hotel, just out of view of the bride in question. The twin staircases curved dramatically toward the second floor, framing the black grandfather clock on the landing. I was half-tempted to grab one of the gothic candelabras from the bureau nearby and challenge my mother to a duel, but that might upset some of our hotel guests.

Then again, a lot of them would probably appreciate the show. We'd always attracted a certain kind of person here—the kind who could probably quote *Rocky Horror Picture Show* word for word and collected jars of moon water on their windowsills. Our guests were a fun, quirky bunch.

The brides who booked their weddings here, however?

That was another story.

Weddings on the sprawling, elegant Underwood Hotel grounds weren't cheap, so we got the occasional entitled brat who had never been told no once in her life. Like this one, who nearly burst into tears when my mom told her we'd have to relocate her ceremony after three straight days of rain turned the grassy lawn at the back of our property into a soggy mess. Her chairs were going to sink right into the mud if we didn't come up with something better.

I was the one tasked with giving this woman a tour of the grounds to choose another location. I wanted to grumble about it a little longer, but she was waiting. Besides, I could probably stand to be a little more grateful I was given a place to land when my life fell apart a month ago.

If it weren't for my mom and dad's generosity, I might still be unemployed. And possibly homeless, for that matter. It wouldn't hurt to dial back the attitude.

I adjusted my grip on the clipboard and held in a groan. With a sigh, I reached up and twisted the ends of my long, dark brown hair and turned to my dad, his wire-rimmed reading glasses perched low on his nose.

"Back me up here, Dad," I said, throwing out one final plea.

But my dad, who avoided conflict like the plague, took a backwards step toward the stairs with a sheepish grin. "I think I'm needed on the third floor," he said, lifting a foot onto the bottom stair. Fred Wheeler was better at handling budgets than people, so it was no surprise he wanted nothing to do with this bridezilla.

I was on my own.

The woman's name was Frances, and her blonde ponytail swung back and forth as I led her out to the courtyard, assuring her we'd find the perfect spot for her ceremony in two days. "Is there no way you can install some kind of flooring at the foot of the hill?" she asked, tempting me to hit myself in the face with my clipboard. "It's just… I had my heart set on exchanging our vows beneath that massive oak tree."

I sighed. "The only way you're going to do that is if everyone wears their rainboots. We could always place straw bales for seating instead of the white chairs."

Frances scrunched up her nose as we walked down the brick path past the gargoyle fountain. "Straw bales? No thanks. This isn't some… country hick wedding."

Right. What was I thinking?

Frances followed me through the rose garden on the south side of the hotel. The blooms were gone, but the landscaping crew was hard at work, tucking in clusters of orange mums and arranging white pumpkins along the path.

Over on the other side of the T-shaped hotel, the pool and hot tub were closed for the season, but the communal fire pit drew a lot of guests in the evenings. We handed out free s'mores supplies nightly, and my parents hired a professional storyteller to scare the guests with tales of the ghosts that allegedly haunted this place.

That area probably wasn't bougie enough for Frances, who let out a frustrated whimper when she caught sight of the chaos on the edge of the garden. Men in holey, faded T-shirts were hauling wooden boards and running orange extension cords across the grass, their power tools echoing off the hotel's stone façade.

With Halloween just a few weeks away, construction was already underway to prep for what would be our busiest weekend of the year. Halloween was Underwood, Michigan's claim to fame. For decades, people had flocked here each October to visit the old lighthouse, said to be haunted by a woman forever waiting for her lover, whose boat capsized in Lake Michigan. The crowds only grew until the town embraced its spooky reputation.

Now, more than 15,000 people visited every year for Halloweenfest. With our hotel wedged between the lake and the five-block stretch of the festival, we had no choice but to join in.

Never one to be outdone, my mom had apparently decided a simple haunted house wouldn't suffice this year. No, she'd hired a crew to build an entire haunted *village* on our back lawn: a bank, a schoolhouse, a library, a doctor's office, and even a mortuary. They were all modeled after photographs of Underwood's Main Street from over a century ago. It was a massive investment, but my dad was confident we'd earn it back. The haunted village would be a permanent installation–Halloween weekend was just the launch.

Frances scrunched up her nose again. "Will all of this construction mess be moved out of the way before Saturday?"

"Yes," I assured her, gripping my clipboard so hard it turned my knuckles white. My heels clicked on the walkway as I led Frances toward the edge of the rose garden. "They'll put a pause on their construction and we'll get everything moved out of the way."

Frances nodded, but she still wore a displeased scowl. "I didn't know it would look like this when we booked. It's honestly a little... tacky."

I bit my bottom lip, wanting to agree with her. The kooky haunted village detracted from the gothic elegance The Underwood Hotel was known for. It was hard to imagine the original owners ever constructing something so garish during the hotel's prime in the 1920s.

"Well, Halloween's sort of a big deal around here," I told Frances as we approached a stone arch. "But don't worry," I continued, "I'll make sure there's no–"

As we stepped through the arch, my words were cut off by a sudden mechanical whir above my head, and something fuzzy and gigantic dropped from above. The second I felt it graze my hair, I shrieked and tumbled backward away from the eight-legged monstrosity. My clipboard went flying and my heel sank into the ground at the very edge of the sidewalk, throwing me off balance.

Strong hands caught me before I hit the ground—one pressed against my upper back, the other supporting my rear end.

It took a second to register that I'd just fallen into the arms of one of the construction crew members. And not just any of them. I was looking up into the green eyes of the foreman, a broad-shouldered man with a permanent scowl and shaggy blond hair that fell over one eye as he looked down at me.

He had a reputation for keeping to himself, heading straight from his room to the construction site each morning without ever interacting with the staff. My mom had a humorous theory that he only spoke in swears, which was what we mostly overheard from across the lawn. My dad just said he admired the guy for minding his own business, complimenting his work ethic.

I hadn't exchanged a single word with this man since his crew checked in and started their work two weeks ago. I couldn't even remember his name.

And yet, his hand was still firmly planted on my ass.

Chapter Two

Cameron

JESUS CHRIST. I WENT over there to reroute an extension cord, not to catch a hysterical woman in heels. She was lucky I was there, too, because the jagged rocks in the landscaping would've bruised her ass.

Then again, she had some extra cushioning there, from what I could feel.

Swallowing, I helped her to her feet on the pavement, hoping my hands didn't linger on her body for too long. Thankfully, she didn't seem that pressed about it. She was too distracted by the ridiculous mechanical spider dangling from the stone arch.

"This has to go. Immediately," she snapped.

It took longer than it should for it to register she was talking to me. Did she think I had something to do with that ugly thing? "Alright, good luck with that," I muttered, picking up her clipboard for her.

"Excuse me?" She didn't take the clipboard from my hands. Instead, she just stared, her mouth agape.

"I've got nothin' to do with this, so you're barkin' up the wrong tree, lady." Since she wouldn't take the clipboard, I handed it to the uppity blonde woman beside her, who looked like she smelled shit or something.

"Aren't you the crew leader?" The brunette put a hand on her hip and furrowed her brows. "I don't care if you're the one who hung this here or not, but you're going to have to do something about it. She's getting married here in two days, and we can't have colossal spiders dropping from the sky."

"Congrats," I said to the blonde one, whose eyes would bulge out of her skull if she widened them any more. And then I turned back to the woman causing my blood pressure to rise. "But like I said, I've got nothin' to do with this. My crew builds. We don't decorate. Someone else is in charge of all this gimmicky bullshit, so I guess you can take it up with the Wheelers."

She drew in a sharp inhale, finally taking the clipboard from the other woman. "Frances, why don't you head around the corner and look at the gazebo area as a potential ceremony location? I'll catch up in a minute."

The blonde one nodded and took off down the walkway, disappearing around the side of the hotel. And then the brunette with the dangerously grabbable butt turned to me with a scowl. "Please don't cuss in front of the guests."

Had I cussed? "I don't think I did."

She scoffed like I was intentionally gaslighting her. "You said 'bullsh it.'"

Oh, right.

I had said that.

"Well, if a grown adult can't handle hearing the occasional expletive, that's her problem, not mine. She looked like she had a stick up her ass, anyway."

And so do you.

I didn't say that last thought out loud. And maybe that was the wrong assumption, anyway, because she pressed her lips together like she wanted to smile but had to maintain a certain level of professionalism, so she couldn't.

"I'd just like to keep her happy, so please watch your language. And, on a more important note, all those extension cords and tools and lumber piles need to be hidden before Saturday morning."

"Hidden *where*?"

"Behind the village would work. Two hundred wedding guests will be roaming the garden, and you'll have a liability case on your hands if they trip over something. Not to mention, it's ruining the aesthetic."

"You're shittin' me."

She just shot me a stern look, and for a moment, I was too distracted by her long, fluttery eyelashes to think of anything else to say. I just knew a man could get lost in those deep, brown eyes. But I absolutely would not be doing that.

I shook away the fleeting moment of attraction and cleared my throat. "Thanks for the suggestion, but I think I'm just going to leave everything where it is unless the Wheelers tell me otherwise."

A smug smile slowly stretched across her face, and despite her pretty little red lips, there was something almost menacing about it. She took a step closer and extended her right hand toward me.

I furrowed my brows. "What's this?"

"It's called a handshake. Wanted to formally introduce myself."

Cautiously, I accepted her hand in mine, taken aback by the contrast in textures. While my hand was rough and calloused from working in construction for more than a decade, hers was soft, smooth, and so small I was almost afraid I might crush it.

"Cameron Fox," I told her, sticking my other hand in the back pocket of my jeans. "Project foreman."

She tightened her grip on my hand, smirked, and said, "Lucy Wheeler. Daughter of Janine and Fred."

My jaw clenched shut.

Well, shit.

Lucy's eyes twinkled in amusement, likely because she knew she had some control over me now. I gave her hand another firm shake before dropping it and running my fingers through my hair.

"Well, Lucy Wheeler, what you're asking me to do is going to add some overtime hours, unless I pull some guys from another project. Could disrupt our whole timeline."

Lucy glanced over her shoulder at the gazebo around the corner, where the twitchy blonde was waiting for her. "You seem like a smart man," she said, turning back to me. "I'm sure you'll figure something out."

"Oh, I'll figure something out alright, but your parents are going to be billed for it."

"Great. Add it to their invoice," she said, backing away with that same self-assured smile. She really thought she had the upper hand, didn't she? Acting like she owned the damn place. But then again, technically, she did.

I felt inclined to mouth off again, but I held my tongue.

"Thanks, Cameron, for being so *very* cooperative," she said, her voice sweet as syrup as she turned on her heel.

That's it.

"Should've just let you fall," I muttered.

Lucy spun back around so fast I thought she might lose her balance again. "What was that?"

I innocently glanced up at the tree just beyond the garden, its golden-yellow leaves swaying in the breeze. "It sure is pretty here in the fall," I said, dragging a hand along the stubble on my cheek.

Lucy stood still for a moment, debating her next words. Ultimately, she decided on sign language instead, double-checking nobody else was watching us before giving me the finger. And then she disappeared around the corner, leaving my heart racing with irritation.

It took a full thirty seconds for me to snap out of it and remember what I'd walked over here for in the first place. I followed an orange extension cord up to the main building before unplugging it and bringing it back over to our work area, where my guys were standing around taking a water break and messing with their phones.

I didn't like the way Derek whistled at me as I approached. In fact, all the guys were grinning like jackasses. Had I missed something?

"Get you a handful of somethin' over there, boss?" Derek asked, lifting his water bottle to his mouth with a sly smile. His curly red hair was damp with sweat.

Hell. Ignoring him, I made my way over to the back of my pick-up truck to grab my insulated water cup. Wesley was already there, sitting on the tailgate with his steel-toed boots dangling. He had brown skin, dark eyes, and a wide, genuine smile—which he flashed at me as I walked up.

"You haven't spoken to a woman in weeks, and you go straight for the ass-grab? Bold move, man."

He tried to give me a fist bump, but I pretended I didn't see it. "Shut the fuck up. Both of ya."

The whole crew laughed, and Derek moved closer to join Wesley and me by the truck. "Who is that woman, anyway?"

I rolled my eyes. "Hotel heiress. Determined to be a pain in my ass. All our asses." I went on, detailing the extra work she wanted us to do. The guys groaned in unison, and a couple of them cursed under their breath. Holden, the youngest guy on the crew, stomped off toward the haunted mortuary, where we'd been hanging exterior panels all afternoon. One by one, the rest of the guys scattered and got back to work.

Only Wesley and I remained, and I felt his eyes on me as I leaned against the tailgate beside him, picking at the hole in my jeans. "That woman's got you all fidgety," he observed.

"I'm not thinkin' about her."

He stared at me with a knowing smile. I'd met Wesley when we were in our early twenties, back when we were both rookies on our first big construction job. We lost touch for a while, but once I started leading my own crews, I tracked him down because he'd proven himself time and time again as the kind of guy you wanted on your team. He didn't need a lot of explanation. Didn't take too many breaks. He just got his shit done and went home.

"It's funny how you go out of your way to avoid women, and one literally falls into your arms," Wesley said with a laugh.

"I don't go out of my way to avoid them."

"Yeah, you do."

"I don't."

"When's the last time you had a date?"

Instead of answering, I took a long swig of water.

"That's what I thought," he said, giving my back a hard slap before sliding off the tailgate. He started walking toward the job site, but he only made it a few steps before turning back around to look at me. "Just promise that if you mess around with the Wheelers' daughter, you don't piss her off bad enough that she fires us all. I need this job, man."

"I'm gonna fire you for sayin' that."

He just chuckled as he walked off, his boots crunching on the gravel that lined the rose garden. I shook my head and looked down at my ripped jeans, running my thumb along the frayed edges.

Wesley wasn't wrong. I *did* avoid women at all costs. But after finding my wife in bed with a strange man in the house I literally built for her, could anyone blame me?

It was easier to throw myself into work. When I was thinking about measurements, materials, and timelines, I wasn't thinking about how, two years ago, everything I'd worked for crumbled into nothingness.

At least one good thing came out of that marriage.

I pulled my phone out of my back pocket and tapped the side button just to stare at the familiar picture on the lock screen. Those blonde curls and ice cream-smeared cheeks were a reminder of why I worked so damn hard. When everything else in my life went to shit, James was proof there was still something good in the world.

That little boy made life worth living.

Chapter Three

Lucy

I ALWAYS WONDERED WHAT drew my grandparents to this once-condemned old place when they bought it and revitalized it fifty years ago. Was it the rumor Al Capone routinely stayed in one of the grand corner suites during its heyday? Was it that magnificent view of Lake Michigan from the upper floors? Maybe it was just the chance to restore a crumbling resort to its former glory.

Whatever the reason, their legacy was passed on to my parents, who took over when I was just a little girl. Back then, The Underwood Hotel was my playground. I could be found ducking behind potted ferns to scare unsuspecting guests, riding the elevator up and down, or stealing flowers from the garden to make crowns for the gargoyles.

Every October, when we were fully booked and my parents became too busy to keep track of my whereabouts, I spent my time pestering the concierge, Alan. He'd send me on "secret missions" to find the most random things, like a guest's missing cufflink, his lucky penny, or a fox he swore he saw in the rose garden.

I never found any of them. It wasn't until I was much older that it dawned on me that Alan was just trying to get rid of me for a little while.

Now, I stood at the window of my third-floor room, coffee in hand, staring out at the water. I could just make out a sliver of the lake between the trees in Hathaway Park across Lakefront Avenue. And from this angle, I had a clear view of the jobsite, which Cameron and his crew had cleaned up—just like I'd asked.

A small victory.

I yanked the damask velvet curtain the rest of the way open to allow more light into my room. With a sigh, I set my coffee on the rolltop writing desk and slipped out of my bathrobe, draping it over a chair.

When I left Underwood for college, I never imagined I'd end up right back where I came from, taking up residence in one of the guest rooms. But a few weeks ago, I lost my copywriting job at a marketing firm in Chicago to an AI bot.

I didn't want to ask for help. Especially after I refused to major in hospitality, like my parents encouraged. Eighteen-year-old Lucy wanted nothing more than to get as far away from The Underwood Hotel as possible. I'd spent my entire life within those walls. I knew every square inch, every creaky floorboard, and every dusty corner of the place. And I'd grown bored of it.

Big city life called my name, and I answered.

Lo and behold, when I was laid off, I came running back to Underwood with my tail tucked between my legs, begging for a job and a room. My parents were gracious about it, of course. My mom acted like this was always the plan, barely able to contain her excitement that we'd finally be working side by side. My dad just handed me a brass key and asked me not to make any permanent changes to the room.

As I tugged on my black pants, I shook my head at the painting of a melancholy Victorian girl sitting on a suitcase on the wall opposite the window. She stared me down every night with her sad, ghostly eyes, and there was nothing I could do about it. That horrible painting was inexplicably bolted to the wall.

"One of these days, I'm going to give you some googly eyes, Mildred," I told her, pulling a satin, beige button-up top from my armoire. I tried to blend in when I worked weddings, drawing as little attention to myself as possible. No bright colors, no loud jewelry, and a toned-down version of my signature red lips.

I was just putting my make-up case away when there was a tap at the door. "Miss Wheeler?"

I smoothed the front of my blouse as I crossed the room. "Coming," I called back, already knowing who it was.

Sure enough, when I opened my heavy wooden door, Marie stood there with a no-nonsense look on her face. Her gray hair was pulled into a tight bun, not a strand out of place, and she wore the same black polo she always did, embroidered with the Underwood Hotel logo. She'd been around almost as long as I had, hired by my parents shortly after they took over.

And, truthfully, after all the years I'd been gone, she probably knew the place better than me.

"We're mopping today, honey," she said. "Make sure everything's up off the floor."

"Marie, you don't have to do that. I can mop my own floor."

Her eyes widened like I'd just suggested mixing bleach and ammonia. "No, no—it has to be done *right.*"

I would have been insulted had it been anyone else saying this to me. But Marie was particular about our hardwood floors, and she took her role as the head of housekeeping so seriously, you'd almost think she'd taken a blood oath to keep everything shiny.

"Why don't you just teach me what chemicals to use? I promise I won't ruin the wood."

"No. I don't want anyone unauthorized touching my mops. Just make sure your floor's picked up."

I held back a smile, knowing I wasn't going to win this argument. As much as I hated letting the staff here treat me like a VIP, I knew better than to challenge Marie. She was the one person in this building whose stubbornness matched my mother's. The two of them butted heads frequently, but my mom loved Marie too much to ever let her go.

And like my mom, Marie still saw me as the irresponsible girl I was when I left this place. It didn't matter that I'd spent eight years managing my own life in the city. To her, I was still that bratty teenager she caught making out with a lifeguard in the laundry room.

(She never told my mom, and for that, I'd always be grateful.)

"The room's good to go," I said, patting my pocket to make sure my skeleton room key was still there before stepping out. "I was just about to head out, too. Big wedding today."

"Oh, that's lovely," Marie said, returning to the laundry cart on the other side of the hall. "Maybe one day you'll be having your own wedding down there in the garden."

"Fat chance. I haven't met a man yet who can handle me, Marie."

She let out a short laugh. "He's out there somewhere. I know it. You just aren't looking in the right places."

"Wrong. I'm not looking at all," I quipped, making her chuckle again as she pushed her cart down the hall. I headed the opposite direction, to the elevator.

Downstairs, Frances and her bridesmaids were having brunch in matching monogrammed pajamas in the bistro by the lobby, and she was laughing, which was a good sign. Outside, the air was crisp, the sky a bright stretch of blue with barely a cloud in sight.

It was setting up to be a perfect day.

I joined the event assistants, Jackie and Delia, in helping the hired florist hang an autumnal garland all around the gazebo. It took us half an hour to arrange all the white folding chairs, and another thirty minutes to tie burnt-orange satin bows on all the end chairs, just like Frances had shown me on her Pinterest board.

"Very nice," her mother said, watching me closely as I moved quickly from one chair to the next. Coming from the wife of a senator, it felt like high praise. And then, during the bridal portraits on the grand staircase, I overheard Frances telling the photographer that having to move the ceremony was a "blessing in disguise" because everything was setting up so beautifully.

For a little while, I started to believe the entire day would go off without a hitch. All the vendors were on time, the reception area on the terrace looked like something out of a magazine, and everything was working smoothly.

I should have expected the other shoe might drop.

And I should have paid more attention to the gray clouds developing in the western sky.

I'd checked my radar at least four times that day, noting how the storms seemed to break up over Lake Michigan. But mid-ceremony, when thunder rolled in the distance, I began to doubt the accuracy of my weather app. And during their vows, when the first raindrop fell on my nose, I immediately took action.

"Jackie, Delia!" I motioned for them to follow me onto the second-floor terrace, where half the reception tables were safely tucked beneath the building's overhang, while the rest were left exposed to the elements. And judging by the heavy sprinkles already hitting my shoulders, a downpour was imminent.

"What are we supposed to do?" Jackie asked, frantically tucking her hair behind both ears. For about ten seconds, I just stood there, hand over my heart, wishing my mom were there that day to tell me exactly what to do and how to do it. But she and my dad were at a conference out of town, and the responsibility fell solely on my shoulders. My eyes scanned the terrace until I spotted the gift table. "Get the gifts. Then the centerpieces. Move fast."

We all sprang into action to move the wrapped presents and card box to the covered section, sticking them against the wall by the DJ booth for now. And then we hurried to protect the centerpieces—little framed pictures of the bride and groom sitting atop vintage books. Despite our frantic speed, everything was getting damp already.

I heard the officiant's rushed voice floating up from the gazebo. "You may now kiss your bride!"

Two hundred people were about to head this way, and only half of them were going to have somewhere dry to sit. The three of us, with help from the catering staff, worked as quickly as we could, dragging all the tables to the covered section as the rain fell. My wet shirt clung to my skin and I could tell my hair was a frizzy disaster, but I didn't have time to worry about that. My heart raced as I attempted to drag the long head table out of the rain. I gritted my teeth and pushed with all my might, the legs of the table screeching against the wet stone.

"Damn it. Come on!" I screamed at it, watching empty wine glasses topple. Where were Jackie and Delia? As rain pelted my face, I briefly toyed with the idea of giving up and quitting on the spot, leaving Underwood behind for good.

That was when I felt the table jerk and glanced toward the other end to see Cameron, his wet hair hanging over his eyes and a gray t-shirt clinging to his pecs. With a toss of his head to get the hair out of his face, he lifted the other end of the table.

"Where did you come from?" I shouted over the sound of the rain.

"Grab that end and lift."

I'd have to get my answer later. Together, we lifted the table and carefully walked it toward the covered area, meandering through other tables and throngs of wedding guests that were now cowering there to get out of the rain. None of them were helping, I noticed—not even the groomsmen, who were already lined up at the bar.

I spotted Frances's big white dress out of the corner of my eye, the soggy train dragging behind her as she walked up the stairs to the terrace. Her face was scrunched up like she was about to cry, but I couldn't deal with her right now.

As Cameron and I moved tables, Jackie and Delia acquired some towels from housekeeping and dried chairs for the impatient guests. I tried not to notice the way Cameron's biceps flexed under his wet shirt sleeves as we moved the very last table, or how unfairly sexy he looked when he ran his fingers through his hair when we were finished.

I stood with my hands on my hips, trying to catch my breath beside him in the back corner near the DJ booth. "What are you doing out here?"

He flattened his wet hair with one hand, his gaze traveling up my body before finally landing on my face. "Saw this all unfold from my window. You were out here looking like a damn drowned rat. As funny as it was, I couldn't just sit there and watch you struggle."

"You thought it was funny?"

The corners of his lips lifted in a playful smirk, but before he could respond, a shrill voice cut through the sound of the rain like nails on a chalkboard. "Are you happy?!"

Frances's hands were balled into fists over her poofy gown, and her frizzy, damp hair framed her reddening face. She looked like a wet poodle ready to bite.

"Frances–"

"Did you not think to check the weather report? My ceremony should have been moved inside!"

I swallowed. "I am so sorry, Frances. I thought the storms were going to miss us. It looked like–"

"They didn't miss us!" Frances stood so close, her spit landed on my cheek. I flinched, but I didn't move to wipe it away. Every pair of eyes in the vicinity, including Cameron's, was locked on the two of us. I couldn't remember a time I felt more humiliated than this.

To make it even worse, the state senator pushed past his daughter, wagging a finger at my face and scowling down at me like I was something he'd scraped off the bottom of his shoe. "I hope you know we're not paying the remainder of our balance on this place. You were woefully unprepared, and it's unacceptable. You should have had a better plan for inclement weather, but instead, my daughter is standing here in a soaked gown on her wedding day."

"Again, I apologize." My legs began to tremble, but I did my best to hold my chin high and look this man directly in the eyes. "We can certainly discuss your final payment at checkout tomorrow."

"No, I don't think so," he said, with his hands in the pockets of his slacks, like this conversation was nothing to him. Like he talked down to women all the time. "There's nothing to discuss, unless you want to speak to my lawyer."

He didn't give me a chance to respond. He just grabbed his daughter by the arm and pulled her away, shaking his head and muttering something about me under his breath.

I was so stunned by the interaction, my legs were locked in place. I curled my toes against the squishy soles of my soaked flats, bile threatening to rise in my throat. I hated how small that man just made me feel, like I was a child getting scolded in front of the whole class. One of the bridesmaids actually laughed, and I felt it burn all the way down to my bones.

Then, I remembered who I was.

And that humiliation turned into rage.

Before they could get too far, I lurched forward and tapped the senator on the shoulder. He whipped around, his brows raised in surprise.

"I understand that you're upset," I said, pausing to take a breath. I glanced from him to his daughter. "I'm sorry that this happened, truly. And I know you're just looking for someone to blame."

His lips parted like he had something to say, but I didn't give him the chance.

"But what I won't do is stand here and let you act like this sudden downpour was some kind of personal failure on my part instead of an act of God, especially when every single person in your wedding party was looking at the same sky and carrying the same weather app on their phones. Anyone at any time could have said 'let's move this inside' and our team would've made that happen."

The man just stared at me with his mouth agape, and Frances blinked rapidly, clearly not used to someone standing up to her father. But I continued.

"If you'd like to bring your lawyer into it, that's fine. We have one, too, and she'll be happy to point out the weather clause in the contract you signed."

Someone let out a low whistle behind me. It sounded like Cameron, but I wasn't sure.

The senator took a step forward, contorting his face into a disdainful sneer. "You little bitch," he muttered, only loud enough for Frances and me to hear.

My spine straightened. I had a dozen insults on the tip of my tongue, but I bit the inside of my cheek and willed myself to keep them in. I wouldn't give him the satisfaction. Instead, I forced myself to take a breath before turning on my heel and walking away.

I shoved through the double doors leading into the building, stepping off the terrace into the dark hallway on the second floor. The only light came from the fake flames on the gothic wall sconces between each door. I knew I couldn't run away from this–the wedding was only half over, and I still had work to do. I just needed a quiet moment to pull myself together.

The doors creaked open behind me, and my whole body tensed, bracing for Frances or her father to come charging in for round two. But the slow, cautious footsteps didn't match the energy I was expecting.

And then I heard Cameron's voice.

"Gotta say, it's a lot more fun to witness you bustin' someone else's balls than it is to be on the receiving end of it."

Chapter Four

Cameron

LUCY TURNED AROUND WITH her palms pressed to her cheeks, her eyes wide with horror like she couldn't believe what she'd just done. "Oh my god," she said, staring at nothing in particular. "I just berated a state senator in front of his entire family."

I walked a few steps closer, throwing a quick glance at the ominous raven painting on the wall. God, did they get some wholesale discount on unsettling artwork, or what? I liked this one better than the painting of a sickly looking boy in my room, at least.

Would the Wheelers notice if I swapped them out?

I returned my focus to Lucy, who shivered and rubbed her wet arms. "My mom's going to lecture me when she hears about this."

"Or congratulate you."

"You don't know my mom. She's all about bending over backwards to please people like them."

"I *do* know your mom," I pointed out. Since starting this haunted village project, I'd met with Janine Wheeler at least half a dozen times to keep her updated on our timeline. She was sweet, but sometimes a little curt. She seemed happiest with me when I understood her vision without needing much explanation.

In fact, I was getting so good at predicting Mrs. Wheeler's preferences, I got a bonus *"I like you"* out of her Friday afternoon when she approved the layout revisions for the schoolhouse.

"And she loves me," I continued, lifting the driest part of my t-shirt to wipe the water droplets from my jaw.

Lucy's eyes lingered on my exposed abdomen for a couple seconds before making the slow climb to my face. Her brows furrowed. "My mom 'loves' you?"

I dropped my shirt, shooting her a smug half-grin. It was more of a reaction to catching her checking out my abs, but I let her think it was about the comment I was about to make. "Oh yeah. I'm a big hit with moms."

To that, she rolled her eyes, but there was the tiniest hint of a smile in the corners of her lips.

I stepped closer and braced one hand on the wall near her head, close enough to catch the scent of rain in her hair combined with something sweeter. Her shampoo? Perfume?

It almost made me forget what I was about to say.

"You know what? I've saved your ass twice now. First in the garden and now on the terrace. And I haven't gotten so much as a 'thank you' out of you either time. Am I going to have to have a little talk with Janine about your manners?"

Lucy shook her head, fighting that smile even harder now. I knew referring to her mother by her first name would get under her skin. "Fuck you," she muttered.

She didn't mean it.

I blinked, feigning shock. "Oh, wow. Point proven."

Lucy drew in a deep breath like she had a scathing comeback, but instead, she slowly exhaled with a stubborn, "Thank you."

And finally, the grin she'd been holding back broke through.

I cleared my throat. "You're welcome. But you owe me."

"Oh, no, no, no," she said, tugging at her wet collar as she took a step back. "I don't like owing people favors. I don't need that held over my head."

Before I could reply, she glanced around before ducking into a room marked *Employees Only*. Ignoring the sign, I followed her into a laundry room, where the smell of detergent was almost overwhelming. I watched Lucy open a cabinet and ruffle around before pulling out a little pad of paper with The Underwood Hotel's logo on it. It matched the one on my nightstand.

"What are you doing?" I asked, letting the door swing shut behind me.

She didn't answer. Instead, she grabbed a pen and scribbled out a note. I waited with my hands in my pockets, curious. She signed her name at the bottom and tore off the top sheet before holding it out toward me. "Here. Take this down to the bar by the lobby and tell them Lucy sent you."

I took the note from her and glanced down at her swoopy cursive writing:

Give this man whatever he wants.

♡ Lucy

"There. Now we're even." She tucked her damp hair behind her ears before crossing her arms. "You should ask for the Room 313 Lager. The Underwood Brewery makes it exclusively for us."

I folded the note and slipped it into my back pocket, grinning. "You think this makes us even?"

"Yes."

"Hmmm." I cocked my head to the side like I wasn't sure. A whole list of sarcastic responses cycled through my mind, but I pushed them all aside, wondering if I could say something riskier.

I could ask her to join me.

The invitation was on the tip of my tongue, and everything about Lucy's body language was giving me the green light to say it. Hell, her nipples were pointing right at me through the thin fabric of her top. And after the day she was having, she could probably use a drink.

But at the last second, I took a deep breath and let the moment pass. I was too fucking scared.

"Okay. This beer better be worth it," I said instead, giving her a little grin as she turned to put the notepad away. We walked back out to the hall together, where I touched my back pocket as if checking that her note was still there.

"Guess I need to get back out there," Lucy said.

"Good luck with all that."

"Thanks. Enjoy your drink." She smoothed out her shirt before retreating down the hallway, hesitating for half a second before pushing open the door. I sucked on my bottom lip, watching her through the tinted glass until she disappeared into a crowd of people at the reception.

I should've asked her.

***

I made it back to my room just in time for James's nightly call. Vanessa's name lit up the screen as I tossed my keys onto the dresser. But it was James's blurry face–half hidden by something gray and furry–that I saw when I answered.

"Hey buddy. And... hi, Smokey."

"Smokey wants to talk to you, Daddy." He had the poor cat in a chokehold, his wiggly legs dangling in midair.

I chuckled, sitting down on the foot of the bed. "Um, Smokey looks like he wants you to put him down. And I'd rather talk to you, James Bean. Whatcha been up to today?"

James Bean was the nickname I gave him when he was a gassy newborn, and for some reason, it stuck. Unfortunately, so did the gas. At four years old, that kid could probably out-fart any of the guys on my crew, which was saying something.

"Mommy took me to the li-berry. Do you want to see the books I got?"

"Of course, buddy."

James darted out of frame, the camera wobbling as he ran across the room. I caught a glimpse of his pajama-clad legs before he plopped back down in front of the screen with a proud grin and a stack of picture books in his arms. He held them up one by one, attempting to read the names of the books.

"And this one is, um..."

He was shaking a lot, but I thought I could make out the title. *"The Goodnight Train."*

"Yeah! And this one's..."

"The Little Engine That Could."

"Yup. And look at this one!"

"Another train book," I noted. "I'm sensing a pattern here. What's with the sudden interest in trains?"

I could hear Vanessa's voice off-camera. "It's the obsession of the week. It'll pass."

I chuckled in agreement, losing my train of thought for a moment as James struggled to hold up the next book, an encyclopedia about locomotives. Because there was a man's voice in the background, too, saying something about how last month, it was motorcycles.

Skyler was there.

That was nothing new. Skyler was *always* there, even more so now that he'd put a ring on Vanessa's finger. There was nothing I could do about it, and maybe one day I'd get over the discomfort of having some man I barely knew hovering in the background, listening in on my bedtime calls with my son. Perhaps someday I'd hang up without wondering what kinds of things Skyler and Vanessa said about me the minute the call was over.

But tonight wasn't that night.

I shifted my weight on the bed and forced a smile as James said, "That's all of them. Mommy said I could only get eight books."

"Eight's a lot," I said, and then I told him all about the little train depot near the hotel. I wasn't sure if it was still in operation or not, but there was a caboose permanently parked outside. "When you're here for Halloween, I'll take you to see it."

That made James screech in excitement, shaking the phone as he jumped up and down. Skyler's voice boomed in the background, asking him to calm down, and I felt a twinge of guilt like my phone call only got him rowdy before bed. I calmed him down by asking about his day at preschool.

A few minutes later, Vanessa said it was time for him to brush his teeth. "Say goodnight to your dad."

"Goodnight, Daddy."

"I love you, Bean."

James said it back, but instead of hanging up, he dropped the phone on the floor, giving me a terrific view of the ceiling fan I'd installed. I smiled from one side of my mouth as my thumb hovered over the red

X, and I heard Skyler say something that made my stomach twist into a knot.

"Pick one of those books for me to read to you, buddy."

I hung up before Vanessa had a chance to pick up the phone. And for a moment, I just sat there and stared at the floor between my feet, resentment and jealousy coursing through my veins.

Not because Skyler had taken my place in Vanessa's bed, which I'd made peace with a long time ago.

But because he was the man tucking in my son and reading him a bedtime story. I should've been grateful. I should've been appreciative that this seemingly decent guy even wanted to step up and be part of James's life.

But all I felt was the hollow ache of missing it myself, and the fear I might get phased out.

Right now, my current arrangement allowed me to see James every other weekend. Kalamazoo was only about fifty miles east, close enough that I could be there in an hour if something ever came up.

My next job, however, was seven hours away in Tennessee, and I'd be there for three months. Maybe longer if the weather didn't cooperate. It was good money, and I liked knowing this work allowed me to provide James with everything he ever needed. And then some.

But this also meant that come November, I wouldn't be able to see him as often. I'd have a week in between to soak up every little bit of him, and then it was off to Tennessee.

I might not see my son again until Christmas.

With a heavy sigh, I fell backward onto the bed. My hands rested on my stomach as I stared up at the bronze, ornate light fixture on the ceiling. I tried to distract myself by calculating how much one of those probably cost, then multiplied it by however many rooms this place had.

It was the kind of mental math that usually settled me. But that night, it did nothing to calm my nerves.

What if he started calling Skyler "Daddy" instead of me?

Sighing again, I dragged my hand down the scruff on my jaw, and then rolled over to reach for Lucy's note in my back pocket. I lay there and stared at it, my eyes following the perfect loops of her handwriting. She'd hate to see the scribbled notes I made on the jobsite clipboard.

I smiled to myself, reading the note again and again.

Give this man whatever he wants.

♡ Lucy

I thought of the way she muttered *"fuck you"* and tried to pretend she wasn't amused by my teasing. I'd made a beautiful woman smile, and for once, I felt like more than just a pathetic, divorced dad.

I rolled over again, stretching toward the nightstand. I wouldn't be taking this note down to the hotel bar like she suggested. Instead, I decided to hang onto it, and I tucked it away in the drawer beside my bed.

She really should've been more specific. Because one of these days, when the timing felt right, I just might cash that note in for something more than a drink.

Chapter Five

It was almost one o'clock when I finally emerged from my room on Sunday. It was well past the guests' checkout time, which meant I could avoid any accidental run-ins with Frances, her father, or anyone else who saw me at that wedding reception.

I rubbed my lower back on the elevator, sore from being on my feet for ten hours and dragging all those tables. The back of my throat stung like I'd swallowed razorblades, but that was probably from shouting over the sound of the rain. I could have stayed in bed all day, but the need to talk to someone besides Mildred was too strong.

That mopey Victorian girl wasn't a good conversationalist anyway.

I knew a conversation with Ronnie and Greta in the bar would fix me right up. When I stepped off the elevator, Greta's voice already drifted down the hall, her rendition of "Hello" by Adele instantly making my skin pebble with goosebumps.

She sat behind a baby grand piano just off the lobby, her red hair styled into perfect waves with a deep side part. Watching Greta perform felt like stepping through a time machine into 1940s Underwood, and if not for the semi-modern pop song she was crooning, I might've actually believed I'd time-traveled.

"She's going to make me cry," I said, hoisting myself up onto one of the wooden barstools. A tiled walkway separated the bar area from the cushy lounge chairs and Greta's piano, positioned in front of the tall, gothic windows at the front of the hotel.

Ronnie, with his impossibly shiny brown curls, had been hovering in the corner to sneakily scroll on his phone. He slipped it into the back pocket of his black jeans and turned around to lean onto his elbows on the bar. "Don't even get me started. I'm going to need an ice bucket to catch all my tears if she sings 'All By Myself' again. I told her she's not allowed to do Céline Dion anymore, but that bitch never listens."

There were only a few guests in the lounge–a man reading the newspaper, a woman knitting an orange scarf, and an elderly couple sharing a slice of pecan pie as they watched Greta perform. When the song finished, they all stopped what they were doing to clap. Greta gave a little bow as she rose from the piano bench before walking over to us.

"Guys, do you see that old couple sharing a slice of pie?" Her eyebrows pulled together like a sad Disney princess as she slid onto the barstool beside mine. "That's the most adorable thing I've ever seen."

"A minute ago, she wiped the corner of his mouth with her napkin," Ronnie said, shaking his head. "Makes me sick to see other people find love."

"You're the worst," I said with a laugh. Ronnie ended things with his ex-boyfriend at the beginning of September, and he'd been regretting his decision ever since.

He turned around to whip up a new drink he was calling a Spiced Maple Bourbon Smash, sliding shot glasses toward Greta and me so we could sample it before he added it to the October drink menu. I loved being one of Ronnie's regular taste-testers.

And this concoction was my favorite yet.

"Does it taste like October?" he asked as we both wiped our mouths.

I shivered as the bourbon made its way down my esophagus. "Absolutely. It tastes like I want to rake leaves in a cozy sweater while listening to Bon Iver."

"Perfect. That's what I was going for... I think."

"It tastes like I want another." Greta slid her empty glass across the bar.

"Only the first one's free, babe," Ronnie said, picking up both our empty shot glasses with one hand. He turned to me. "Same to you, even if your last name's Wheeler."

I just laughed. Ronnie and Greta were my two favorite people at this hotel, taking me under their collective wing the second I came crawling back to Underwood. Ronnie said they had to determine I wasn't a "snobby heiress bitch" first, but I guess I'd proven myself worthy of their friendship.

"Hey, Ronnie," I said, sitting up a little straighter. Trying hard to appear casual, I avoided looking him in the eye. "Did one of the construction guys come down here last night with a note from me?"

"A note?"

"Yeah, for a free drink."

"No. But Keylee was working, too. I feel like that's something she would've mentioned, though."

Greta folded her arms on the bar. "You giving out free drinks to the construction guys?"

"Well, just one in particular." I shifted on my stool, crossing my legs at the ankles. I could still remember how Cameron smirked at me the night before, propping his hand up on the wall with that cocky confidence of his. It gave me the impression he probably flirted with women all the time, but it still made me a little weak in the knees. "The foreman—that quiet, tall, blonde guy with the muscular forearms? He helped me move some tables last night when it started raining, so I just, you know, wrote him a little 'I owe you a drink' note."

The other two exchanged looks, and then Ronnie gently touched my arm. "Luce, are you fucking stupid?"

"What?"

"When a construction man with sexy forearms helps you move furniture, you don't send him to the bar alone. You escort him there. And then you take him up to your room and let him lay some pipe."

Greta just nodded with a grin, her gold hoop earrings catching the light from the stained-glass lamp at the end of the bar. "He's totally right, especially if you're talking about who I *think* you're talking about."

"Okay, first of all, the guy's a little too smug for my taste. And second, I'm not going to hook up with a contractor my parents hired. That's not a good idea."

Ronnie scoffed. "That's what makes it so fun."

They spent the next several minutes giving me advice about Cameron, insisting I needed to invite him to the bar for drinks. Like I'd even dream of bringing him around those nosy little gossip goblins. I laughed off every suggestion, doubling down on my refusal to even entertain the idea. This went on for a while, until I realized I was probably keeping both of them from their work.

"You two need to get a hobby," I said, pushing off the bar as I slid down from my stool. "See you guys later."

"One day, you'll be a whore just like us!" Ronnie called out after me as I walked away.

I heard Greta gasp. "Hey! Speak for yourself."

"I'm speaking for both of us, and you know it."

Greta paused for a beat, and then she let out a sigh of resignation. "Yeah, you're probably right."

***

I had every intention of returning to my room to water my plants and read a book under a blanket on my balcony, but that was before I smelled the maple pecan fudge wafting from the candy store in the hotel.

Just off the lobby, one corridor of The Underwood Hotel was dedicated to a row of quirky shops, almost like a shopping mall. It felt like a village within a village, attracting locals and tourists as much as our hotel guests. The candy store at the end was known for its decadent homemade treats, including the seasonal maple pecan fudge, which I'd devoured with sticky fingers ever since I was a little girl.

And after being called a "little bitch" by a weaselly politician, I deserved a little treat. So I turned down the corridor and made my way past all the other stores–the bookstore, boutique clothing shops, a Halloween store, and a stationary shop. By the time I reached Crescent Candies, I was practically salivating.

The shop clerk told me I'd arrived just in time to snag their last batch of the day. She threw in one of their new butterscotch caramels for me to sample, too, and I couldn't be sure if this was something they did for all of their customers, or if perhaps she recognized me as the Wheelers' daughter. "You're my new favorite person," I told her on my way out.

Just as I stepped into the corridor, I saw a person emerge from The Bookish Owl out of the corner of my eye. I paid no attention to them until a husky voice said, "How does one become your favorite person?"

My breath caught in my throat. Cameron walked my way with a white plastic sack dangling by his side, wearing a black Detroit Lions hoodie.

I stopped, allowing him to catch up to me before we continued down the sunlit corridor together. "By giving me sweets," I answered, looking over at his face as our steps fell in line.

Cameron's jaw clenched like there was a risky comment threatening to spill out at any second. But he only said, "What kind of sweets are we talking about here?"

I held the box up, waving it near his face. "Free Butterscotch caramels. But I'm more excited about this maple pecan fudge."

"Maple pecan fudge," he repeated slowly. "Sounds a little too sweet."

"There's no such thing."

We passed the boutique storefronts, our footsteps echoing off the black and white tile. Neither of us were in any hurry to get anywhere. And when I reached a set of double doors leading to the courtyard, I turned to him and asked, "Are you heading this way? It's kind of a shortcut to the elevators."

Cameron hesitated, shooting a quick, subtle glance in the direction of the lobby. "Yeah, I am."

He followed me as I pushed through the doors, the air outside cool and crisp against my face. I pulled my cardigan a little tighter around my body. As we followed the diagonal path across the garden, where wet, golden leaves clung to the bricks, I caught myself staring at Cameron's face. There was a little scar at the edge of one eyebrow that I wanted to ask him about, but that felt too intrusive.

So I settled for a safer question. "What book did you get?"

He turned to me with a lopsided grin that made my heart pitter-patter. I could practically see the gears turning in his head as he worked on a sarcastic response. "*Dealing With Fussy Hotel Heiresses for Dummies.*"

I smiled back. "Can I borrow that when you're done? Sometimes I can't deal with myself."

Cameron sucked air in through his teeth like he was about to deliver some regretful news. "Sorry, I already told that senator he could read it next."

I gasped and shoved Cameron so hard he tumbled off the brick path, nearly falling into the thorny, dead rose bushes. When he rejoined me on the walkway, we were both laughing. "Hope there was a chapter in there about not provoking an heiress when you're next to a thorny bush. Jerk."

"I haven't read that far yet. Clearly." He straightened himself, tugging on the bottom of his hoodie, and his grin never faded. When Cameron smiled—when he *really* smiled—a dimple formed on his right cheek, giving him a boyish charm I hadn't noticed before. It made it hard to look away.

We reached the dead center of the garden, where the gargoyle fountain stood tall with water trickling from the creature's mouth into the wide basin below. When I was a little girl, I always imagined this gargoyle coming to life, flapping his enormous wings and busting through the fourth-floor windows to snatch guests out of their rooms. It didn't look so scary now.

As we neared it, I held out the box from Crescent Candies. "Do you want to try one of these?"

Before he could answer, I sat down on the ledge of the fountain and took the lid off the box anyway. It didn't matter if Cameron wanted to try one or not—I couldn't wait any longer.

He backed up against the fountain and slowly sat down, holding the sack from the bookstore between his legs. I sat the open box between us on the ledge, tucking the lid beneath it. Each golden-brown cube of fudge was topped with a single glazed pecan. "I've been obsessed with these since I was a little girl," I said, carefully picking one up with two fingers. "They're my favorite thing about fall."

Cameron reached for a piece, and for a moment, we both chewed our fudge in silence, with only the sound of trickling water and the breeze around us. "Okay, I get it now," he said, holding his fingers to his bottom lip after he swallowed.

I laughed before eating the rest of my piece. I offered him a second one, and he accepted it, shaking his head like he was disappointed in himself. I decided not to tease him about it. "The sugarplum truffles they make at Christmas are almost as good. Not quite, but almost."

"Does your hotel go all out for Christmas like you do for Halloween?" Cameron asked, nodding in the direction of the haunted village.

The words "your hotel" caught me by surprise. This place didn't exactly feel like *mine*. I just lived here. And worked here. And shared DNA with the owners.

That's all.

"Not quite," I said. "It's more peaceful at Christmastime. In the winter, we kind of lean into the whole old-fashioned Victorian Christmas vibe. Sleigh rides and carolers, that kind of thing. And the snow in this courtyard is always so beautiful, especially when it's still untouched and sparkly. It's the closest thing to magic I've ever seen."

I was rambling, but Cameron didn't seem to care. He'd listened to every word without interrupting, his eyes focused on mine the entire time. "That sounds... amazing. Like something out of a Dickens novel."

"It truly is."

For a moment, neither of us said anything, but it was a comfortable silence. Our knees were close enough that I could feel the heat from his leg radiating through the fabric of my jeans. I didn't move, and neither did he.

I put the lid back on the box of fudge, shifting even closer to him without really meaning to. "Speaking of novels, are you going to tell me what book you actually bought, or is it a secret?"

Cameron took a slow, deep breath and wiped his hand on his jeans without saying a word. For a moment, I regretted asking him this question—maybe it was too personal. Maybe it was some kind of self-help book. Maybe it was something he was embarrassed to be reading. What right did I have to know?

But he cleared his throat and reached into the bag. And then he pulled out a brightly colored picture book with an illustration of a train on the cover, its smoke forming the title: *All Aboard the Haunted Train.*

My lips parted in confusion, and I could feel Cameron studying my face closely. I assumed the book was for a nephew or something, but I decided to make a joke anyway. With a smile, I teased, "Do you need colorful pictures to get through a book? That's adorable."

"It's for my son," he said.

Oh.

He's a dad.

And just like that, my heart fluttered in my chest and my lungs forgot how to work. Clearly there were more layers to this man than I'd guessed, and I wanted to peel back every single one. My ovaries were already melting, but I needed to know more.

Was he a *good* dad?

"You have... a son?"

"Yeah. He's really into trains right now. And books." He tore his eyes off my face to stare at the cover of the book, licking his lips. His expression morphed into an almost vengeful scowl, which didn't quite make sense until he said, "And I'm going to read this one to him over

FaceTime tonight so his future step-dad can stop stealing my thunder at bedtime."

Chapter Six

Cameron

I HADN'T MEANT FOR my mention of James to be some big revelation. But Lucy stared at me in stunned silence, studying my face like she was piecing me together. Figuring me out. I could tell she was seeing me differently now, and I was surprised by how much I cared.

"His name is James." I leaned forward to pull my phone out of my back pocket to show her the photo on my lock screen. "Here he is forgetting that ice cream goes in his mouth, not on his face."

"Oh my god," Lucy said, letting out a short laugh as she touched the bottom of my phone, her fingers resting on my thumb. The softness of her touch made it hard to think about anything else. "He's so cute. And my goodness, he looks exactly like you."

She hadn't realized what she'd just admitted, so I decided not to point it out. My cheeks felt warm as I opened up the photo app and quickly navigated to the pictures I took of James last weekend, when Vanessa forgot to send his pajamas with him to my brother's house, which was where we lived during my weekends in Kalamazoo. James had to sleep in one of my old Rogers Construction t-shirts. It skimmed the top of his feet, and he hated the whole thing until I told him it made him an honorary construction worker. I had to let him use my tape measure to check the length of his bed before he'd go to sleep, but it did the trick.

I told Lucy all of this, watching her face to see how she'd react. And it was difficult to tell, but I thought there might have been tears welling up in her eyes when I got to the part about the tape measure.

"That's incredibly sweet. You seem like such a good dad."

I swallowed hard and slid my phone back into my pocket. Lucy didn't know that in just a few weeks, my next job would be taking me farther away from James than I'd ever been. Could I still be a good dad from such a long distance?

"I just try to do my best," I said.

"Will he ever get to come here, to The Underwood?"

That made some of the tension ease from my shoulders. I sat up a little straighter, and my smile returned. "Yeah. For Halloween, actually. He gets to spend that whole weekend here with me."

"Seriously? He's going to have the best time! We'll have so many activities for kids. And do you know about Halloweenfest?"

I shook my head.

"Oh God, just wait. The whole town goes all out for Halloween, taking over downtown with this massive carnival, and we're so close to the festivities that it kind of spills over onto the hotel grounds. It's going to be insane."

"James is gonna love the fuck outta that."

Lucy let out a gentle laugh, reaching up to tuck her hair behind her ears with both hands. A sudden breeze undid her effort, blowing her hair back in front of her face. It made the air smell like an unexpected mixture of maple and coconut, though only one of those scents came from the candy between us. The other one was entirely Lucy.

A group of blackbirds caught Lucy's eye at the edge of the garden, giving me the chance to stare at her face without being obvious. I just took her in quietly; her long eyelashes, the slight upturn of her nose, and the beauty mark by the corner of her mouth that reminded me of an old Hollywood star.

Fuck, she was beautiful.

The second I sensed her turning to face me, I looked down and nonchalantly slipped James's book back into the bag.

"Cameron."

Her quiet voice made my heart skip a beat. It was a wonder I was able to choke out a response at all. "Yeah?"

"Why didn't you cash in that note for a free drink at the bar last night?"

I should have known she'd follow up on that. For a second, I thought I might fib and say that I did, but Lucy knew better. And something about those big, beautiful eyes made me want to be honest, even if it made me seem a little pathetic. "I figured as long as I keep it, you'll still owe me a favor."

Lucy pretended to be offended, but her smile gave away her true feelings. "That's not how it works."

"Guess you should've clarified."

"And just what do you think this 'favor' is going to be?"

I let the question hang in the air for a second, delighting in the way her eyes lit up when she looked at me. With a smirk, I leaned over and bumped my shoulder against hers to be playful. "I'll think of somethin'."

"Is your mind going to a dirty place right now?"

I just laughed. I couldn't answer that. Because I wouldn't lie to Lucy, and my answer might earn me a slap. Of course my mind had gone there. I hadn't actually *meant* anything sexual by saying she still owed me a favor, but now all I could think about was what this woman looked like naked.

Instead of saying any of that out loud, my eyes wandered to the gargoyle at the center of the fountain with a stream of water flowing from its mouth like projectile vomit. That got my mind out of the gutter pretty quickly.

I twisted back around and folded my hands between my knees. The plastic handle on the sack from the bookstore killed my wrist, but I didn't do anything about it.

A heavy sigh slipped out of my mouth. In just a few weeks, I'd be packing up and relocating to Tennessee, and The Underwood Hotel would simply fade into a memory. And that was the story of my life. Always moving on, always starting over. Never making any real connections with people, and certainly not with a woman like Lucy. It could only lead to hurt.

If not for me, for her.

So when I looked up and caught her eyes flitting to my lips, I pretended like I didn't notice. Instead, I focused on the pinecone on the ground between my feet, tapping the toe of my boot against it. I acted like it was the most interesting thing I'd ever seen, refusing to even glance in Lucy's direction. I simply couldn't.

"You know, you're really beating the hermit allegations," she said.

I looked up. "Hermit allegations?"

"You've got a reputation for hiding up in your room, only going to the jobsite and back. But now I've seen you outside two days in a row."

I let my gaze fall to Lucy's red lips, but only for a couple of seconds. If they lingered there too long, I might be too tempted to lean in and kiss her. With a quick glance at her eyes, I returned my focus to the pinecone and swallowed hard. "Well. It's easier to avoid forming attachments with people when you keep to yourself."

Out of the corner of my eye, I saw Lucy shift on the ledge, tucking her hands beneath her legs. I braced myself for questions, but they never came. Lucy just understood.

After a moment, she picked up the little box of candy and held it on her lap. "I should probably get back inside. I do laundry on Sundays."

I rose to my feet and turned around to offer Lucy my hand. Not because she needed help getting up, but because I wanted an excuse to touch her. She accepted it, letting her fingers linger on mine just a second longer than necessary after she stood up. I told myself it didn't mean anything.

My eyes drifted up toward the top of the hotel, where its pointy spires stood out against the pale gray sky. I'd never had the opportunity to work on a building like this, and I probably never would. You just didn't see Gothic Revival style structures going up anymore, especially not in the Midwest. Everything I'd worked on lately was some variation of the same damn thing: a boring box with a roof on it. Newer builds with actual craftsmanship and character? Those were hard to come by.

I dropped my gaze to the woman beside me, her dark hair blowing in the gentle breeze as she tucked that damn box of candy beneath her arm like it needed to be protected. I watched her hug herself as she tilted her head back to observe the clouds. Finally, she turned back to me, letting out a nervous chuckle once she caught me staring. "What?"

"Nothin'." I kicked the pinecone away as we began our walk toward the hotel. "Just thinkin' about how hard it's gonna be to leave this place."

Chapter Seven

Lucy

THE BOOKSHELF NEAR THE lobby had always felt like my own little secret, even though it was in plain sight. It was tucked off to the side of one of the staircases, and only a handful of our guests ever paused to peruse the books.

Once, a guest even asked me if the books on it were *real*.

On Monday afternoon, I found myself standing in front of it with my fingers trailing along the spines just like they did when I was a little girl. Back then, I would take a stack of books to the fireplace in the lounge and sit on the rug with my dress spread all around me as I flipped through them from cover to cover. Books about ghosts, Victorian interior design, the Great Lakes—whatever my parents picked up from local thrift stores. The only children's books were classics like *The Velveteen Rabbit* and *The Wind in the Willows*.

I could probably still recite my favorite scenes word for word.

That afternoon, I was looking for something specific. And I found it on the top shelf, its red spine catching my eye. *A History of the Underwood Train Station*.

I stood on my tiptoes to pull it down and turned right to the photo I remembered best, a full-page spread of passengers leaning out the windows of an old steam train, waving goodbye to people on the platform. Frozen in time.

"Lucy Mae Wheeler."

I snapped the book shut, my heart jolting at the sound of my full government name coming out of my mother's mouth. God, talk about being transformed right back to my childhood.

I turned around. "Yes, Mother?"

Her laptop rested on one arm as she walked my direction from the reception desk, her heels clicking on the tile. "Did you 'disrespectfully accost' the senator?"

It was only a matter of time before that came up. I held the train book against my chest, picking a piece of lint off my skirt with my other hand. "He's just a *state* senator," I mumbled.

My mom peered at her laptop screen over the top of her reading glasses and scrolled. "Did you humiliate him in front of his friends and family?"

I could deny it, or I could proudly own up to it. I decided to go for the latter. What was she going to do, fire her own daughter? "Yeah, and I'll do it again. Bring 'im in."

"Lucy."

"Bring his daughter, too."

"Lucy! These Yelp reviews can make or break someone's decision to stay here."

"Good. Maybe we don't want the kind of guests who would side with a politician over a drenched woman just trying to do her freakin' job." I paused, closing my eyes for a second. I couldn't forget the patronizing way that man wagged his finger at me after I'd just busted my ass moving furniture in the pouring rain. "He accosted and humiliated me first, Mom. I simply stood my ground."

She lowered her laptop and stared into my eyes like she was trying to decide whether to believe me or not. Was she seeing me as her daughter right now, or just an employee?

I took a step closer.

"You always taught me to stand up for myself when I'm wronged, and that's exactly what I did. And I did it with a charming smile, the same way you would. I learned from the best."

I'd just pulled the *"I learned it by watching you"* card, and I was afraid I'd pushed this too far. But I watched my mom's face soften, the concerned wrinkles in her forehead flattening under her silver-streaked auburn hair. "I hope you didn't catch a cold."

I was twenty-seven years old, and my mom was still worried about me catching a cold. She'd probably bring soup to my room, or at the very least, send someone upstairs with some.

After realizing the senator's Yelp review didn't make a dent in our positive rating, she decided to let it slide. Both of us got to work, reviewing the event schedule for the week and ensuring everything was set up and properly staffed.

My mom noticed the *Underwood Train Station* book on the back counter while grabbing something from the printer. "What's this for?"

I had no idea how to answer that question. I barely knew the answer myself. I just knew I couldn't fight the compulsion to look for that book after Cameron told me his son loved trains, and in the back of my mind, I wondered if the boy might enjoy it as much as I had when I was little.

Probably not. I was a weird one.

And I hadn't made up my mind about giving it to Cameron yet. When he said he avoided forming attachments, I took it as a subtle warning: *don't get too close to me.* I got the impression he was laying down a boundary, and perhaps offering this book to his kid, whom I'd never met, was crossing it.

Then again, it was just a book. I would've done the same for any other guest at this hotel who told me their child was obsessed with trains. Just last week, I let a little girl take home one of the bumpy gourds from the display on the reception desk. I was just being extra hospitable, and giving this book to Cameron for his son wasn't any different. Right?

My mom blinked at me, waiting for an explanation. "Oh. I'm gathering some research for the next hotel newsletter. Thought I'd really dive into the history of the town."

It wasn't a complete lie. I was assigned newsletter duty not long after I came back to Underwood, which made sense, considering my background in copywriting. And I *had* thought about mentioning the train depot in the next email, hoping to entice past guests to come back and explore the parts of town they might've missed the first time.

"I do love your newsletters." My mom raised her glasses to the top of her head. "Just make sure you're promoting the haunted village. We've invested too much into it to let people miss it."

I was about to tell her that nothing killed the vibe of a good story faster than a sales pitch, but I didn't get the chance. The sound of shuffling footsteps and wood knocking together distracted us both.

Virgil, the groundskeeper, walked by the reception desk carrying his rickety wooden ladder, his slight limp more noticeable than usual. He was wearing his usual denim button-up shirt, and his combover had flopped to the wrong side again, bouncing as he walked.

"Afternoon, ladies," he said with a nod.

My mom always joked that Virgil "came with the building," something her parents used to say. He was the building's caretaker while it was sitting vacant–the only person who kept the boiler running and the pipes from freezing in the winter. He knew this place inside and out, and after all that time, it had become more than just a job to him.

That was probably why he was so reluctant to retire, no matter how many times my parents gently nudged him toward the decision. Even his wife showed up sometimes, standing behind him with her hands on her hips while begging him to come home for the night. Once, she told us she was the "other woman" in her marriage because Virgil's heart belonged to The Underwood.

None of us could argue with that.

We returned his greeting, and then he grunted to adjust the ladder against his side. "Finally replacing the bulbs in the sconces down here," he said.

I held my breath as he turned down the hall, and beside me, I could feel my mom stiffening. "That man's going to break a hip," she whispered. She pinched the bridge of her nose and closed her eyes. "I think it's time to have a tough conversation with him."

"Mom, don't," I blurted, surprised by my own urgency. "Just... not yet. It'll break his heart."

My mom exhaled, shaking her head. "It's time. It was *time* ten years ago, Lucy. Things aren't getting done quite right lately, and it's because he's just not physically able to do them anymore. I know this place won't be the same without his presence, but we can't risk him getting hurt just because we're sentimental."

I knew in my heart she was right. I just couldn't stand the thought of having to force him out. He'd retire when he was ready. At least, that's what I'd keep telling myself.

That evening, as I made my way down the long hall past the guest rooms on the first floor, I couldn't help but notice the glow coming from the antique sconces seemed slightly... off. When I looked up, I observed that every other bell-shaped shade was tilted at a strange angle, carelessly replaced without realizing they weren't aligned.

My mom was gone for the day, but if the shades were still crooked in the morning, she'd probably take it as another sign it was time for Virgil to go.

It took me ten minutes to find a stepladder, and another five minutes to track down a Phillips head screwdriver. One by one, I adjusted every single crooked sconce. It wasn't an easy task for a woman in a pencil skirt with minimal upper body strength, but I got the job done.

As I worked on the last one, the construction guys started heading down the hall toward the elevator, exhausted and sweaty at the end of their work day. Every single one of them gave me a polite nod or *hello* as they passed. One of them even offered to help, but I assured him I had it under control.

Their voices disappeared around the corner and the elevator dinged before carrying them up to their rooms. I stayed perched there on that step ladder, taking my time with the last screw.

I was stalling, really. Cameron and I hadn't spoken all day. I'd spotted him positioning the roof trusses over the haunted mortuary, but he was busy, and we didn't interact. But now that the rest of the crew had clocked out, that meant he had to be close behind.

And there he was.

I heard the heavy thud of his workboots before I saw him. Without even looking up from the sconce, I knew it was Cameron. I *felt* him. The energy in the hallway shifted as his footsteps slowed behind me.

My stomach was already fluttering, but when I looked down and saw Cameron's crooked smile, I nearly fell off the ladder. His hair messily fell across his forehead, and he adjusted the strap of his lunchbox as he rested a hand on it. For a fraction of a second, his eyes flicked to the back of my skirt, but he snapped them back up to my face just as fast.

"Well, aren't you just Little Miss Do-It-All," he said, scanning the other sconces in the hallway like he was assessing my work. "Thought this was more of a Virgil kind of job."

My lips parted as I carefully stepped down from the ladder. "You know Virgil?"

"Oh, yeah," Cameron said, lifting the fingers from the top of his lunchbox in a casual gesture. "He knows where every pipe and wire's buried out there. Nice guy. Reminds me of my grandpa."

And there was yet another layer of Cameron's personality I hadn't seen before. Little by little, he revealed the softer parts inside him, adding some nuance to the gruff man I met in the garden.

"You're full of surprises, Cameron Fox."

"What's that mean?"

I just shook my head as I pushed the stepladder against the dark wainscotting, thinking of that train book behind the reception desk. As I looked up into the green eyes of the man who said he didn't like forming attachments, I felt a tiny nudge in my heart. Just a *little* push to show him that there was no risk in letting me get to know him a little.

"Wait here a second. I have something for you."

His eyebrows lifted. "Okay..."

I hurried toward the front and tossed the screwdriver on the desk, promising Marci, our young night receptionist, I'd be right back. She barely looked up from the book she thought she was hiding behind the monitor.

A minute later, I returned to the hall holding the heavy book close to my chest. Cameron was still standing there just outside Room 139, looking up at the detailed plasterwork in the ceiling until he saw me. He watched me approach with curious eyes.

"I, um—" I held out the book. "This is for you. For James, actually."

He took it slowly, his lips parting as he glanced at the crimson cover with the words *The History of the Underwood Train Station* pressed in gold foil.

"I used to love this book when I was little," I said, unable to control the nervousness in my voice. "I'd sit in the lobby and read it from cover to cover, over and over again. I would flip through the pages and just make up stories in my head. About the people on the train. Where they were going. Who they were leaving behind. I was an imaginative little weirdo."

He gently flipped the book open like it was a valuable antique. And he was quiet, so I kept rambling.

"I'm not sure if James will like it or not. But maybe it'll mean something since it's connected to where his dad works. That's kind of cool, right?"

Cameron looked up, and he still didn't say a word.

My heart plummeted straight into my stomach. Oh God. I'd crossed a line. This was too much. I should've just left it on the desk and used it for my next newsletter instead of forcing a connection with someone who explicitly stated he didn't want that. He kept to himself for a reason.

The longer he was silent, the more my brain spiraled.

Cameron leaned over and put the book down on the top shelf of the stepladder. Was he refusing to accept it? Before I had time to sputter out an apology, his lunch box slid off his shoulder and dropped to the ornate rug beneath our feet.

And then he took a step forward, grabbing me by the waist with both hands. He paused for a heartbeat, as if to make sure I wanted him this close, and then he lowered his mouth all the way down to mine with a force that stole the breath right out of me.

The way Cameron Fox kissed me wasn't patient. It wasn't hesitant. He kissed me like a man starved, and I was hungry, too.

I opened my mouth to taste him and fully let him in. Rising to my tiptoes, I arched backward while sliding my hands up his solid chest. I liked what I felt there, all hard muscle beneath soft cotton. His body curved with mine, and one hand lifted to cradle the back of my head. For a man so hesitant to form an attachment, he sure was holding me like he already had.

"Damn it, Lucy," he whispered between kisses, pulling back just enough to look into my eyes. For the first time, I really noticed the gold flecks in his irises before he touched his forehead to mine. "You pulled me in."

"I'm sorry." I swallowed.

Cameron's arms wrapped around me tighter and he kissed me again, slower this time. And that kiss told me what I needed to know: that he *wanted* to be pulled in. He'd just needed a little coaxing.

Just down the hall, a doorknob turned with a loud *click*, followed by the squeak of old hinges. Cameron and I broke apart from each other, wide-eyed and breathless, as a man emerged from Room 135 and muttered a hello before turning the other direction. My cheeks were burning.

Cameron cleared his throat and reached for the book on the stepladder. "Um. Thanks for sharing this," he said, his voice lower now. "I'll show it to him when he's here."

"You're welcome," I managed to say, still trying to catch my breath as he bent to retrieve his lunch box from the floor. When he stood again, he looked straight into my eyes and then just past me, watching the guest continue down the hall. There was the faintest smile on Cameron's lips.

"Think he saw us?"

I looked over my shoulder at the guest, whom I'd seen around a lot the past couple of days, and then turned back to Cameron. "That guy's only interested in one thing, and it's the complimentary muffins in the lobby. He doesn't care about us."

Cameron let out a little chuckle as he pulled out his phone. He glanced at it and said, "I need to head upstairs. James is going to call any minute.

His gaze lingered on my face for a moment. I just nodded, trying to resist the urge to apologize again. Reaching up to tuck my hair behind one ear, I finally said, "I'll see you tomorrow, then."

"Yeah." He licked his lips, looking down at the book. "Yeah, I'll see you tomorrow."

I watched him go until he disappeared into the elevator alcove. And as I folded up the step ladder and headed back toward the lobby, I could still feel the ghost of Cameron's kiss on my lips.

Chapter Eight

Cameron

As a young kid, anytime I'd scrape a knee or an elbow, my dad would say, "Bring me a hammer and hold your thumb out on the table, and I'll help you forget all about that knee, kid."

Then he'd let out this deep, booming belly laugh like it was the funniest thing in the world, and I'd get so mad I'd punch his leg until I really had forgotten about the scrape.

God rest his wisecracking soul.

I hadn't thought about that in years. Not until Tuesday morning, when my hammer slipped and I drove it straight into my own damn thumb like an amateur.

"Son of a bitch."

Pain shot straight up the bone, and blood was already pooling beneath my thumbnail. I gritted my teeth, shaking my hand out.

Of course this happened now. I'd just chewed Derek out for half-assing the siding on the haunted schoolhouse because he was too busy scrolling on his phone. Letting my ego take over, I'd picked up a hammer to show him how it was done.

And this was what I got for it. A bloody thumb that throbbed with every heartbeat.

"You good, boss?"

I ignored Derek's question and tossed the hammer on the ground with a sigh. "We've got four weeks to complete this job. And we're going to do it right."

Wesley raised an eyebrow at me as I turned around, but he didn't say a word. I walked around to the other side of the row of half-constructed haunted buildings, needing a minute to collect myself.

Four weeks.

That's how long I had. Come November, The Underwood Hotel, this town, and the people here would be hundreds of miles away. And I kissed Lucy without mentioning a word of that.

I should have walked right past that tight little skirt and gone right up to my room. I should've just taken a cold shower and reminded myself that no matter how beautiful and sweet she was, she wasn't mine to touch.

It wasn't like I'd committed to anything. Lucy knew when my contract ended, and she kissed me back. But I couldn't shake the feeling like I'd left something important unsaid. Most people don't pack up and move three states away when a job ends. My failure to mention that felt a little... disingenuous.

Lying by omission.

My phone buzzed in my back pocket. I grunted, knowing I should ignore it after the confrontation with Derek. But just in case it had something to do with James, I pulled my phone out and checked.

Vanessa: The preschool is having parent teacher conferences next Thurs evening, and I can't get anyone at the hospital to trade shifts with me. I'm sick over this. Is there any chance you can make it?

Cameron: Yes. I'll make it work. Send me the info.

I wasn't even aware preschools held parent teacher conferences. What the hell was there to discuss? The fact that he still wrote the letter S in his name backwards? His reluctance to share his favorite toys? I grinned to myself as I put my phone away, grateful I was close enough that I would probably only have to leave work an hour or two early to make it.

My damn thumb throbbed. The best way to forget about it—and everything else on my mind—would be to get back to work, so I made my way around to the front of the village and picked up the hammer I'd thrown. When I straightened, I was distracted by some movement over in the garden.

There Lucy was, holding up her phone like she was taking pictures of the hotel. I sucked in my bottom lip while I watched her crouch down to get a better angle. I couldn't be sure, but it looked like she was trying to include some flowers in the foreground of her shot.

I glanced at my crew. They were all busy or just trying to stay out of my way after the hammer incident. Not a single one of them noticed me slip away.

"Look out, Ansel Adams," I muttered as I approached her.

She sprang up quickly, almost dropping her phone. "God, you scared me."

"Shit. Sorry."

"No, it's okay. I'm easily startled."

I took a step closer. "What are you taking pictures of?"

"The hotel. I'm trying to get some creative shots for our next newsletter, but I'm no photographer."

"Let me see."

She stepped in close, lifting her phone between us. Shoulder to shoulder, we both looked down at the screen, but I could barely register the images as she swiped through them. I was too busy thinking about the way she smelled, how the side of her arm mashed against mine, and how warm I suddenly felt.

Look at the pictures she's showing you, dumbass.

"Go back."

Lucy listened, swiping back to the photo she'd just passed. The stone raven perched on the edge of the birdbath was in focus in the foreground, framed by the arched windows of the hotel behind it. "This one?"

"Yeah. If you're going for spooky, that's perfect."

She peered up into my eyes. "So it's newsletter-worthy, then?"

"Definitely. Post it."

My eyes flicked to Lucy's parting red lips. If it weren't for the couple walking hand in hand on the other side of the garden bed and my crew hammering away nearby at the jobsite, I might have kissed her right there.

Maybe it was a good thing we weren't alone. I wouldn't be able to keep my hands to myself. Not with the way her olive green pants hugged her ass.

"Have you ever been to our conservatory?" Lucy asked, motioning toward the glass structure at one end of the building. "It's the quietest place in this hotel."

For a second, I thought she was just making conversation. I followed her gaze toward the arched glass, where the sun reflected off the ivy-covered panes. But when I looked back at Lucy, she was already watching me, and I understood she wasn't just spouting off fun facts.

"Uh, no... I haven't."

"Do you have time for a quick tour?"

No, I didn't have time for a tour or whatever else Lucy was hinting at. I had flooring to install, materials to unload, and a crew who couldn't be trusted to cut a straight line without someone breathing down their necks.

"Yeah, show it to me."

***

"I think it was Professor Plum, in *here*, with the candlestick," I said, folding my hands behind my back as Lucy led me down the rows of mums and marigolds inside the conservatory.

She let out a bubbly, genuine laugh at my stupid joke. "I used to make the concierge play Clue with me when I was a little girl," she said.

"Don't you need three players for that?"

"Not the way I played."

I nodded, pretending to understand. "Uh huh. And did this concierge enjoy the game as much as young Lucy did?"

"No. I think he wanted my parents to send me to boarding school."

It was my turn to laugh. We came upon an enormous pot of dirt, and the words on the brass plate in front of it caught my attention. "Corpse flower?"

Lucy crossed her arms, making her cream sweater pull tight across her chest. "Yeah, it's dormant now, but it blooms every seven years, and the flower smells like rotting flesh."

I turned to her and blinked. "Wow. You're really setting a romantic tone here, Wheeler."

She grinned. "Just be glad it's is dormant."

"When will it bloom again?"

"In another couple years, I think. I missed it last time."

"How unfortunate."

"It's actually—" She stopped short, her gaze dropping to my hand. "Cameron, what happened to your thumb?"

I looked down at it like I'd forgotten it was even there. The nail had already started turning an ugly, deep shade of purple, making it appear even worse than it felt.

"Ah," I said, wiggling my thumb just to feel how bad it still hurt. "Hammer. Happened just before I saw you. Still fuckin' hurts."

I chuckled at myself, but Lucy winced. I was about to put my hand in my pocket to hide it when she reached for it, wrapping her soft fingers gently around mine. Without a word, she lifted my hand to her face, inspecting the bruised nail closely as she traced her thumb along the edge of mine. And then, holding my gaze, she brought my thumb to her mouth, resting it on her bottom lip. I held my breath as she pressed the gentlest kiss to the swollen skin next to the nail.

My entire body went still.

This was somehow both the sweetest and hottest damn thing a woman had done to me. She never broke eye contact, and I didn't dare tear my eyes away, either. I couldn't remember the last time a woman had been so nurturing and gentle with me.

"You should be more careful," she said, her lips vibrating against my thumb.

Careful? I think fucking not.

I slipped my hand out of hers and brought it to her cheek, trailing my fingers down her jaw. Then, I held her face with both hands, holding her in place as I closed the gap between us. She sighed against my mouth, and I felt it all the way to my bones. I kissed her slowly, touching my lips delicately against hers like she might break. But when Lucy fisted the front of my shirt and tugged my body closer, I lost all control.

"God, Lucy," I whispered, sliding a hand down the curve of her back. I let it linger on her ass for a second before my palm drifted down her thigh, coaxing her leg upward until her knee lifted and pressed against my hip. She let out a soft gasp when I squeezed her thigh, leaning her backward over the stone wall bordering the marigolds.

My lips trailed down her jaw to her neck, and her leg tightened around me, pulling me flush against her body. My hips ground into hers. It was almost too much. Too good. Too... dizzying.

"Lucy, you should..." I dragged my bottom lip across her collarbone. "You should know that... I'm leaving after this month."

"I know."

I pulled back just enough to see her face, my arms still wrapped around her waist. "I mean—I'm going to be hundreds of miles away in Tennessee, and I don't know where this job will take me after that."

Lucy just stared. I didn't even know if I was asking her to stop or giving her permission to keep going. I just knew this needed to be said. Lucy deserved to understand exactly what she was walking into.

"In November, I'm gone," I continued. "And you won't see me again."

I knew the weight of those words as I said them. And maybe they were harsh, especially as she was underneath me against that stone wall with my saliva on her lips and my groin pressing against hers in a way that left nothing to the imagination.

I just needed her to know she had an out before this went any further. We could close the door on this right now before it started to mean something.

Lucy's hands slid down my back until they cupped my butt through my dirty work jeans. "Then I guess we need to make October count," she said, flinging that door wide open.

Chapter Nine

Lucy

"You might've heard of the haunted lighthouse in Underwood, Michigan, but what you might not know is that just blocks away, the historical Underwood Hotel has a few ghost stories of its own."

The dark-haired girl in the lobby spoke into her boyfriend's camera as he walked backwards, angling his shot to perfectly frame her in front of the double staircase. They'd asked permission to film some content for their YouTube channel earlier that afternoon, a courtesy not all ghost hunters and influencers bothered with.

Guests like this came through all the time, getting in everyone else's way and poking around places they shouldn't. But these two seemed to be just as interested in the history and architecture as the alleged paranormal activity, and they were charmingly nerdy enough to get away with it. I didn't mind watching them film while I worked on the newsletter at the front desk.

"There's a full moon tonight," Marci muttered, leaning onto her elbows down at the other end of the desk. She blew some loose strands of teal hair away from her eyes and shot a worried look my way. "How many emergencies do you think we'll have?"

During the last full moon, the bathtub in Room 212 overflowed and leaked into Room 112, and a drunk guest started a fight in the bar. I couldn't blame Marci for being a little superstitious. Then again, she was always going on about the moon and the alignment of the planets.

"Emergencies? Hopefully zero," I answered.

"The Muffin Man hasn't been down here yet tonight. Maybe he died in his room."

"Stop," I said with a laugh. "Nobody's dying here tonight. And if they do, call my mom. I'm..."

I wasn't sure how to finish that sentence.

Before Cameron and I slipped out of the conservatory earlier that day, I whispered my room number in his ear. It was an invitation. He seemed to understand the message, pulling me in for one last kiss and repeating the number back to me. "*Three twenty-seven.*"

Marci and I weren't close enough to talk about that kind of thing, so I told her I was taking a sleeping pill and turning in early after a long day. Just because I was on site didn't mean I had to handle everything that came up.

Not tonight.

I took a quick shower when I got up to my room, having taken my "everything" shower the night before. Then, I changed into a cropped white t-shirt and some comfy, loose black pants, not wanting to be too obvious. And hell, he might not even show up.

But just in case he did, I dimmed the lights and lit a candle–which definitely wasn't allowed–letting its cozy pumpkin spice scent fill the room. That sparked an idea for exclusive Underwood Hotel candles in our gift shop, so I grabbed a notebook and sat on the bed to scribble out a plan.

And at 9:07, there was a light knock on the door.

My heart jumped to my throat and my notebook slid off the bed. "Coming!"

I padded across the hardwood floor with my bare feet and yanked the door open. Cameron stood in the hall, freshly showered, his damp hair pushed back and a clean black T-shirt stretched across his chest.

"Hey," he said, giving me a closed-lip grin as he chewed a piece of gum, his jaw flexing in a way that shouldn't have been as sexy as it was.

"Hi." I pulled him into my room before a guest had the chance to see us. He took it all in—the candle, the tower of books against the dresser, and my open notebook on the floor. With his hands in his pockets as he stepped through the room, his eyes stopped on the painting of the sickly Victorian girl with her sad, sunken eyes.

"Aw, is that a portrait of you as a little girl?"

I swatted at his stomach with the back of my hand. "No, you jerk. I named her Mildred."

Cameron shook his head as he took in the girl's vacant stare. "I don't think I like Mildred. Who do I speak to if I want to make a complaint about the unsettling decor in this place?"

"Me."

We stood face-to-face between my bed and the dresser, close enough that he could have reached out and touched me if he wanted. But his hands stayed firmly in his pockets. It was hard not to notice his stiff shoulders or the way he took a long, slow breath as he looked around the room. Was he nervous?

"Can I get you something to drink?"

"No, thank you," Cameron replied.

"Are you hungry?"

"No, I ate a while ago." His eyes darted around the room some more until they found mine. "Unless you wanted to eat, I mean. I could eat."

"No. I had dinner before. I…" I let my voice trail off, realizing mid-sentence he didn't need to hear about the microwave dinner I wolfed down before my shower. "I'm not hungry, either."

God, this was brutally awkward.

We both knew why he was here, but at this rate, it was going to take hours before either of us made a move.

Cameron tensed up even more, like he wasn't sure what to do with his body. I kept waiting for him to make some other sarcastic comment about my room, but he didn't. Finally, he let out a loud exhale and ran a hand through his hair. "Sorry. I'm not very good at this."

"At what?"

"Being alone with a woman. It's been a while, and I think I forgot what to do." He paused to chuckle at himself, putting his hand back in his pocket. "Pretty pathetic for a thirty-two-year-old man, isn't it?"

I chewed on my bottom lip as I took in his boyish face, the faint shadow of stubble, and the way his black tee somehow made his green eyes even brighter. "Cameron," I said, my voice low and soft as I let his name linger for a second. "You wouldn't be standing in this room right now if what you were doing wasn't working on me."

He grinned at the floor. "I'm not sure what I did. Wasn't I kind of an ass?"

"Not entirely," I teased, glancing toward the armchair, where my white chunky knit blanket was folded neatly over the back. I remembered what Marci said about the full moon, and I got an idea for something that might ease his nerves. "Would you like to sit on the balcony under a blanket and look at the stars with me?"

His lips parted. "Yeah. Okay. That sounds nice."

Draping the blanket over my arm, I opened the door to the balcony I shared with everyone else on this side of the third floor. The wrought iron lampposts lit up the garden below, and the sound of the trickling gargoyle fountain carried up to us. The YouTubers from the lobby earlier were outside laughing and filming videos down there. But besides them, Cameron and I had the night to ourselves.

I dragged a metal lounge chair closer to my door and straightened the faded maroon cushion. Cameron eyed it with skepticism as I sat down, squeezing to one side so he could sit beside me. "Are you sure we can both fit on that?"

"Only one way to find out."

As he carefully lowered himself onto the lounge chair beside me, I tried to make room by swinging one leg over the side. The second my thigh hit the armrest, the whole thing wobbled violently before tipping all the way over. I rolled right onto the concrete in slow motion, and Cameron tumbled down on top of me. It was a gentle but clumsy fall, and we landed in a heap on the balcony, laughing so hard neither of us could manage to pull ourselves up.

"Well," Cameron said, his voice a little strained as he shifted his body. His belt buckle pressed against my tailbone. "There's our answer."

Chapter Ten

Lucy

As it turned out, tumbling out of the lounge chair was exactly what we needed to shake the nerves away. In our second attempt, Cameron sat first, parting his legs to leave a space for me to lean back into. I carefully slid backwards into the space, easing down until my back met his warm chest. I pulled the blanket over our legs, tucking it in around us, and his arms wrapped around my waist from behind.

"Is this okay?" he asked.

"It feels nice. Perfect, even."

His grip around me tightened, and I settled against him until I was fully relaxed. Leaning my head back against his shoulder, I finally looked up at the big, bright moon above, partially hidden behind the swaying branches of a tree.

It was the calmest I'd felt all day.

"The night sky didn't look like this when I lived in Chicago," I said.

"When did you live there?"

"I just moved back last month after spending about nine years there. I was laid off from a marketing firm, and long story short, that's why I'm here. I went from writing ad copy for major brands to... making brides cry."

Cameron blew air from his nose in a quiet chuckle. His chin grazed my shoulder. "You're good at this, though. Not making brides cry, I mean, but running things around here. Seems like you're pulled in a lot of directions."

How did he know? I tugged the blanket up higher toward my chin, and sighed. "I am. I don't even have an official title. I mostly do all the things my mom doesn't want to deal with anymore."

"Are you unhappy here?"

I opened my mouth, but no words came out. Was I really that unhappy? I hadn't asked myself that yet. Coming back to Underwood was never part of my plan. I always thought I was meant to be somewhere loud and busy, eating Thai food out of a styrofoam container in my little studio apartment a hundred miles from home.

But here I was, right back in the place I swore I'd never return to, under a blanket with a man I barely knew but kind of already trusted.

"No," I finally answered. It felt like a confession. "I miss certain things about my old life, but being home isn't all bad. Aside from the occasional disgruntled bride or elevator malfunction, the slow pace around here has done wonders for my anxiety."

"I'm sure the maple fudge helps with that, too," he teased. "Saw the empty box on your nightstand."

I chuckled, feeling a little embarrassed. "You weren't supposed to notice that."

"I'm honestly disappointed. That's the real reason I'm here tonight."

"Oh, is that so?"

"Well." He adjusted his arms, and the edge of his wrist grazed the underside of my breast. I could tell it was an accidental nudge, but he didn't pull away. "It might just be half the reason."

"Maybe I'll bring you some tomorrow. But you'll have to share with your crew, or it'll look suspicious."

Cameron swallowed. "I'm afraid of what some of those guys might say to you if you walk up to the jobsite."

"I can handle it."

"I know. I'm just not sure if I can."

My breath hitched, and I turned my head to look at his face. His eyes were already on me, and something about his soft smile made my heart ache in the best way. Without hesitation, I stretched upward to kiss his lips. Cameron leaned in without missing a beat, kissing me back like he'd been waiting all night to do this. His tongue tasted faintly like spearmint, stroking against mine in a way that made heat pool deep in my belly.

God, I was in so much trouble with this man.

When we pulled apart, Cameron pressed his forehead against my temple. "If any of my guys so much as look at you wrong, they'll be the ones walking around with bloody thumbs tomorrow."

A slow smile stretched across my face. I couldn't remember the last time a man had made me feel so protected. So... claimed. The thought alone made my head spin.

"How's your thumb, anyway?" I asked, shifting to look down.

Cameron pulled his hand from beneath the blanket and held it up for inspection. His thumbnail was an angry shade of purple now, but the rest of his nails caught my eye. They were all clean and freshly trimmed, looking nothing at all like the fingernails of a man who worked construction.

"Looks worse than it feels," Cameron said. He tucked his hand back under the blanket, only this time, it landed lower on my abdomen than before. His fingers grazed the skin between my shirt and the waistband of my pants.

And that's where his warm hand rested as he detailed some of his worst on-the-job injuries, threatening to show me a picture of a gash in his calf that required seven stitches.

"Don't think I won't flip this chair again if you show me a picture of your bloody leg," I warned. His laugh vibrated through me as his hand crept up a little higher on my stomach. "How'd you get the scar on your eyebrow?"

His roaming fingers came to a stop, and he inhaled slowly, his chest rising against my back. There was a pause, just long enough to make me worry I'd triggered a bad memory for him. "My dad," he finally said. "He accidentally hit me with the corner of the trunk when I was helping him unload groceries. I think I was seven or eight. Had blood runnin' down into my eye and everything. My dad cried in the ER because he felt so guilty. We were both cryin'. It was a whole mess."

I laughed. "That's actually really sweet."

"He was a good man."

Was. "Your dad passed away?"

"Yeah, when I was twenty-one. Lung cancer. Caught it too late, so it took him pretty fast."

My heart sank. The thought of losing a parent so young left me scrambling for something comforting to say, knowing the words would never be enough. "God, Cameron. I'm so sorry."

"No, it's okay. I mean, I have my moments, but it's been so long that I just cope with dark humor now. I've got dead dad jokes for days."

"Oh. That's... good?"

He chuckled. "Yeah, so don't apologize. But I just killed the whole romantic vibe we had going here, didn't I?"

I ran my hand down the length of his solid forearm beneath the blanket. "Are you kidding? I'm on a balcony underneath a blanket with a good-looking man gazing at a big, bright moon. The vibe's still there, Cam."

I couldn't see his face, but I felt a puff of air from his lips as he let out a quiet laugh. "'Cam'," he echoed in amusement, trailing his fingers along the side of my waist. It tickled so much I screeched with laughter as I arched my back. He breathed out another chuckle and did it again. I yelped and squealed so loud it echoed off the stone building—and if anyone was still down there in the courtyard, they probably suspected someone was getting murdered.

After a few seconds, the tickling ceased and Cameron brought his warm, rough hand back to my abdomen. He splayed his fingers out on my belly beneath my shirt again.

"Who gave you permission to call me 'Cam', huh?"

"I gave myself permission."

"Then I get to choose a nickname for *you*." His thumb brushed against the underside of my breast through the thin cotton of my bra.

"Some people call me Luce," I offered.

"Short for Lucifer, I assume," he teased, lazily cupping his fingers around my boob. It was almost like he was trying to distract me from the insult.

"You think I'm the devil?"

"I sure did the first time we met."

"You're awful," I laughed out. I tilted my head backward to look at his face. Cameron was already smiling at me, his eyes drifting from one of mine to the other. I stretched my neck, meeting him halfway for another kiss. With his tongue in my mouth, his fingers worked their way upward until they pushed the cup of my bra out of the way. His thumb grazed my nipple first, and then he rolled it between two fingers until it stiffened from his touch.

"This... is the perfect ending to a long day," he whispered against my cheek. It sent a shiver down my entire body. If he was still nervous, he wasn't letting it show at all now. There was confidence in the way he dragged his lower lip across my skin, breathing down my neck.

With his left hand preoccupied, his right hand drifted lower on my stomach until his fingertips tucked just underneath my waistband. He paused there, as if asking for consent.

And I didn't want to leave him guessing.

I arched against him, raising my hips just enough to give him some non-verbal encouragement. And, less subtly, I lifted my knees to part my thighs. I felt Cameron smile against the side of my face as his fingers inched lower.

"You are truly diabolical," he whispered. While pinching my nipple between his thumb and forefinger, his other hand slipped under my panties, bringing his middle finger dangerously close to the sensitive bundle of nerves that awaited his touch. My brain couldn't decide which sensation to focus on, so it simply melted into mush.

The first swipe of his finger along my slit had me gasping in the cold night air like I'd never been touched there before. With his finger wet from my arousal, he circled it around my clit, making me squirm between his legs.

"I've got you," he whispered, pressing a desperate kiss against my temple while he teased my sensitive bud with two fingers. After a moment, he slipped the tip of one finger inside of me, pulling back to look in my eyes as it sank even further.

Cameron didn't rush. He wrapped his left arm around me tight, pinning me there between the blanket and his body while curling his finger in a slow rhythm that made my thighs tremble. His thumb brushed over my clit again and again, and I had to squeeze his forearm to stay grounded.

"Ffffuck." The word slipped out of me as I bit down on my bottom lip, trying to hold myself together.

"I could make you come just like this, couldn't I?" he murmured, his voice low and rough. "But then again..." When Cameron added a second finger, my thighs instinctively tightened around his hand. I reached behind me to curl my palm around the back of his neck, desperate for something to hold onto to anchor myself. Every movement of his hand chipped away at my control until it was all I could do not to scream. I gasped out a needy whimper, digging my nails into his skin.

Cameron's left palm slid over my mouth to muffle me as his lips brushed against my earlobe. "There's someone on the balcony below us," he whispered, "and you're making it really obvious what I'm doing to you under this blanket."

I whimpered into his hand, my body betraying me as I clenched around him. But he kept going, relentlessly curling his fingers deep inside me while his thumb circled my clit. The pleasure spiked until I couldn't stay still at all. My hips jerked against his hand, my thighs shaking as I fought the desperate noises rising in my throat. Cameron held me tight, shushing me while his palm pressed firm over my mouth so no sound escaped.

And at last, the tension inside me broke, and I tilted my head back against his shoulder, moaning helplessly against his palm. My whole body trembled, clenching and pulsing around him while he worked me through every wave until I was broken and breathless under the blanket.

Only when the last aftershock faded did he finally slip his fingers free from inside me and loosen his grip on my mouth. I sucked in a shaky breath, the chilly night air filling my lungs as Cameron's hand slid around to my hip. For a moment, I just sat still, allowing my heart to slow down.

But I was overcome by the need to take back control. I quickly twisted around until I was straddling Cameron, whose wide, eager eyes were exactly the reaction I'd hoped for. The blanket slid down my back as I brought my mouth to his in a kiss, his hands squeezing into my hips like he never wanted to let go. His tongue slid over mine as I ground down against the hard length straining beneath his jeans.

And then my phone rang, and we both went still.

It wasn't my cell, which was sitting on the writing desk just inside. The shrill ring came from the hotel phone, meaning someone at the front desk needed me. Now.

I tipped my head back with a groan, scowling at the full moon. "Why?!"

Chapter Eleven

Cameron

LUCY SCRAMBLED OFF MY lap, dropping the blanket on the balcony on her way back into the room. I scooped it up, following her inside. Her phone, like the one in my room, was one of those old-fashioned rotary phones that looked like it belonged in a museum. The day I checked in, I noticed a little card beside it with instructions on how to dial out–because who the hell knew how to use a rotary phone anymore?

"What's up, Marci?" I heard Lucy ask. I watched her face scrunch up with concern as she slowly lowered herself to the bed. "The whole building? Have you checked the–?"

As the person on the other end spoke, Lucy tilted her head forward, resting it in one hand. I had a feeling our night together had come to an end. Whatever this was, it sounded like a big problem.

"Did you get a hold of Virgil?"

While she spoke on the phone, I folded her big, fuzzy blanket and draped it over the chair in the corner.

"Right, he probably took out his hearing aids for the night." After a second, Lucy sighed, closing her eyes. "And I don't blame you for being scared to call my mom. I get it. Um... let me see if I can contact an emergency plumber. I'll be right down."

She hung up the phone and flung herself backwards on the bed, covering her face with both hands. "Remind me to leave town next time there's a full moon."

I sat down on the edge of the bed next to her. "What's going on?"

"There's no hot water in the entire building. Five guests have complained so far, and there's none in the kitchen or the bar either. And Virgil's not picking up his phone."

Frowning down at the rug below my feet, I thought back to the day Virgil showed me the breaker box in the basement. The old boiler down there seemed to still be in operation, clanking, hissing, and heating the room to a level that felt like the surface of the sun. I was dying in that basement, but the old man had just stood there talking my ear off, completely unbothered.

I looked over at Lucy, her hands still covering her face as she lay on the bed. "Do you have backup water heaters, or just the boiler?"

"Honestly? I have no clue," she said, slowly sitting up again. She ran her fingers through her mussed hair and sighed. "I'm going to try to contact an emergency plumber. If I can even find one who knows how to work on an ancient boiler like ours."

"Could I take a look at it?"

Her brows pointed inward. "Do you know anything about boilers?"

"Just a little," I admitted. I'd picked up a few things when I was doing renovations in an old elementary school a few years back. I was no boiler expert, but I was pretty good at figuring out how to make broken things work again. I liked the challenge. "Just let me see if it's something simple, and I could save you some time... and your parents some money."

Lucy liked the sound of that.

The next thing I knew, she was leading me down the creaky steps to the boiler room. Immediately, I noticed how quiet the room was.

No clanking. No hissing. And though it was still uncomfortably hot, it wasn't *quite* at the melt-your-face-off level, like before.

There were a couple of incandescent bulbs dangling from the ceiling, but I still needed my phone flashlight to get a better look at the boiler. I made my way around the contraption, attempting to find some kind of panel. As I tried to make sense of it all, Lucy began fanning herself.

"You should feel right at home down here, Lucifer," I said, tossing her a wink as I moved around to the other side of the boiler. She didn't reply, but I caught her trying to hold back a smile before I turned back to the job at hand. I did my best not to let the memory of her writhing on my lap distract me.

When I crouched down, I spotted a little door near the bottom of the boiler and, with some effort, forced it open. Inside, the pilot light was out, covered with a thick blanket of dust. It hadn't been cleaned out in a very long time, and that was exactly the problem.

I stood up. "Pilot light's out. I need a long-handled lighter. Maybe a curved one?"

"Isn't this dangerous?" Lucy stood with her hands on her hips, a crinkle forming between her brows. "What if it blows up?"

"Hey, have a little faith in me. Help me find a lighter, and you won't have to deal with any angry guests."

She hesitated, but then she started glancing around. "Well, this room is basically Virgil's home away from home. If he's got a long-handled lighter, it'll be down here. With... everything else."

The old desk in the corner was cluttered with tools, jars full of nails, a completed crossword puzzle, and an overripe Honeycrisp apple. Every surface in the room held random things Virgil had decided to keep, just in case.

It took us a minute to find what we were looking for, especially since we didn't want to intrude on the man's private space. Lucy eventually spotted a lighter in a low cabinet.

Then, it took me three attempts to light the pilot, but the third try finally rewarded me with a steady blue flame. Lucy clapped behind me like I'd just pulled off some magic trick, and the sound sent a warmth through my chest. I rose to my feet, a little relieved that I hadn't fucked this up in front of her.

"Is it actually working?" she asked, stepping closer.

Water began to gurgle through the pipes, and something about the sound of clanging metal coming from deep inside the boiler told me things were back in operation. "It sounds like it. It might take an hour or two for hot water to reach all the rooms, but it's on its way."

She threw her arms around my shoulders, grinning from ear to ear. "You, sir, are my hero right now."

"Nah, anyone could've done that," I said, tucking the lighter in my back pocket so I could put my hands on Lucy's waist.

"Don't try to be humble. You saved me from having to call an emergency plumber. I mean, you prevented me from having to bother my *mother* with this."

I sucked in my bottom lip, looking down into Lucy's bright brown eyes. If only there were a way to explain how good it felt to solve a problem for her thirty minutes after making her come. The room felt hotter than the pits of hell, but with her looking up at me like that, I could've sworn I was in heaven.

And though we stood in the center of a grimy, sweltering basement that smelled like dust and hot metal, I still wouldn't have traded it for my cool and comfortable room upstairs.

Because she was *here.*

If every night for the rest of my stay at The Underwood Hotel went exactly like this, I'd consider myself pretty damn lucky.

***

"All I'm saying is I'd let that bitch sing me to sleep every damn night," Derek said, grinning as he adjusted his grip on the other end of a two-by-four. "Hell, with those tits, she wouldn't even need to sing. Just let me fall asleep between 'em and I'd be out like a baby."

His crude comments about the lounge singer were met with laughs all around as we framed the crooked façade of the haunted mortuary. The guys were paying more attention to him than they were to the task at hand, and it was pissing me off.

I slid the beam toward Derek with a little more force than necessary. "Pretty sure calling her 'that bitch' is the fastest way to guarantee she'll never touch you."

At that, Wesley guffawed, and Derek muttered something under his breath, scrambling for a line to defend himself. Before he could, movement at the edge of the jobsite caught my eye.

Mrs. Wheeler stepped over an extension cord in her tall brown boots, one hand adjusting the glasses atop her head. "Wow, you guys, this is really coming along!"

I nodded for Wesley to take the board from me, then made my way across the grass to where Janine stood with her hands on her hips. "Morning. We're framing the mortuary façade now, and then the bank."

She gave our work an approving nod. "And you'll have it done by the thirtieth?"

"Absolutely."

Janine crossed her arms against her chest, taking time to really look at my face. "Mr. Fox, I came out here to thank you for last night."

That earned a couple of not-so-subtle cheers from the guys closest to me. *Jesus.* I mentally begged them to shut the fuck up as Mrs. Wheeler continued.

"You shouldn't have had to do that, and honestly, it probably shouldn't have even been allowed. That's not what you were hired to do."

Shit. Guilt churned in my gut, knowing Lucy had probably gotten chewed out over this. "I sort of twisted Lucy's arm into letting me take a look at it."

Janine gave me a slow nod, and I prayed my story matched whatever Lucy told her. "Yes, she mentioned she found you in the lobby. How long did it take you, about an hour? You can add that to this week's bill."

"Oh." I shuffled my feet in the muddy grass. "No, I'm not gonna do that."

Mrs. Wheeler's brows lifted in surprise, like this was the first time she'd ever been told no. It wasn't a look of disgust or annoyance, though—it was one of admiration. The corners of her mouth turned up slightly as she concentrated on my face. "I'm sorry?"

I looked right into her eyes, the same warm brown as Lucy's, just sharper around the edges. "I'm not billing you for that. It took two minutes."

"But your knowledge and skill are invaluable. You saved us a lot of trouble, and I'd feel better if you'd let me compensate you. And if not through Rogers Construction, then at least personally."

I shook my head. "Won't be necessary."

Janine's smile grew. Hopefully that meant she was backing off, because I could go round and round with her all day and it'd only be a waste of time. "You're a stubborn guy, aren't you?"

I let out a chuckle. "I've been told that once or twice in my life."

"Well, I'm just as stubborn, Mr. Fox, and you can't prevent me from slipping a restaurant voucher underneath your room door. I know where you live."

What was it with Wheeler women and their insistence on making things even? I let out a defeated sigh, holding back a grin. "Fine, I'll accept that."

She lingered for a moment with her arms folded, her eyes scanning our half-finished structures at the edge of the garden. "Nice work here. You're very skilled with your hands."

I reached up to rub the back of my neck, smirking down at my steel-toed boots.

Yeah, your daughter thinks so, too.

Chapter Twelve

Lucy

THE CONSTRUCTION CREW FLOCKED to me and my box of maple pecan fudge like seagulls on a dropped basket of fries. "Damn," one of them groaned when he took his first bite. After he swallowed, his second "damn!" was even more enthusiastic.

All around me, sweaty men in faded forest green hoodies elbowed past each other to reach into the box with their dirty hands like this was the highlight of their entire day.

"Holy shit, did you make these?" A man with curly red hair licked his thumb before going in for a second piece of fudge. At this rate, there wouldn't be any left for Cameron, who carefully made his way down a ladder by the haunted mortuary.

"They're from the candy store inside the hotel," I answered, laughing at the way one of the man moaned as he took a bite. "Am I going to have to bring more tomorrow?"

"You should make this a daily thing," one of them said, and the others murmured in agreement. I looked past them at Cameron, who strolled toward us with a sexy half-smirk that made my knees weak.

Before he got close, Wesley glanced from him to me and back again. He was the only one of these men who had shaken my hand and introduced himself before reaching for a piece of fudge. "We better get back to work before Cam chews our asses out," he said, nodding for the others to follow him back to their work area. "Thanks, Miss Wheeler."

His warning did the trick. The rest of the crew scattered like schoolkids who'd just been told the principal was coming. There was this calm sense of authority about Cameron that, for reasons I couldn't explain, made my heart flutter.

And something else fluttered between my legs when he got closer, filling the space next to me with his warmth and that outdoorsy-but-clean smell I was starting to associate with him. "Hi," I said, peering up into his eyes as he leaned across my body to reach for a piece of fudge.

He popped it into his mouth and chewed, never once taking his eyes off my face. "Hi. Do I need to kick any of their asses?"

"They were all perfectly respectful."

"That'd be a first." He wiped his hands on his jeans before pulling out his phone to look at the time. Then, he glanced toward the front of the hotel, where mid-afternoon traffic on Lakefront Avenue was a little slow. "Got time to take a walk with me? Maybe in that park across the street?"

I'd been about to ask him if he wanted to sneak off to the conservatory for some privacy. Even on a weekday like this, there were always people roaming Hathaway Park. If he was hoping to steal an intimate moment in the middle of the day, it couldn't happen over there by the lake, where everyone and their mother walked their dogs.

Then again, who was I to turn down an autumn walk in the park with a man who looked at me like I was the only thing he could see?

"Sure," I said, setting the box of fudge on down on an overturned bucket. "But I should go grab a sweater. Let me just–"

"Wait here a sec," Cameron said, already turning away. He walked to the back of the haunted village, where a blue pick-up sat in its usual spot, and pulled something out of the cab. A moment later, he pulled out a forest green hoodie, holding it up as he returned to me. "Can a hotel heiress wear a hoodie, or does it ruin your aesthetic?"

I took the Rogers Construction sweatshirt from his hands with a roll of my eyes, though I couldn't help but grin. "I wear hoodies, Cam."

"Just sayin'. I've never seen you in one."

To make him shut up, I pulled it over my head, inhaling his clean, sandalwood scent as the soft fabric slid over my face. A couple of his crew members were watching us, but Cameron didn't seem to care or notice. He only stared at me with a quiet, proud grin as I smoothed my hair down. There was a hint of possession in that gaze, and I'd be lying if I said I didn't like it.

We made our way around the edge of the garden, past the wrought iron fence that bordered the hotel, and stepped onto the brick crosswalk on Lakefront Avenue. Halfway across, Cameron reached for my hand, and we jogged the rest of the way to avoid an impatient cab driver trying to make a left turn. I threw my head back and laughed as he yanked me toward the curb.

Cameron didn't let go of my hand in Hathaway Park. The path led us between rows of maple trees, their bright red leaves scattered like confetti all across the ground. The park sat high above the beach below, and just beyond the narrow strip of sand, Lake Michigan stretched out before us. The Underwood Lighthouse looked so small from here, but its bold black and white stripes still stood out against the gray sky.

"This was always one of my favorite places," I told Cam as our interlocked hands swung between us. "I didn't realize until now how much I missed this park."

"James is going to love it when he visits. Of course," he said, shaking his head, "he'll be devastated when he learns it's too cold to swim."

"You'll just have to bring him back next August. That's when the water is perfect." I squeezed his hand, and Cameron looked down at me with that warm, sweet smile, the kind I never would've guessed he had in him when we first met.

What happened to that grumpy man who cussed every third word? Was all of that just a front, or was this?

He shook the windblown hair from his eyes before looking down at me, completely relaxed and unguarded, like walking by the lake with me was exactly how he'd dreamed of spending his break. Something about the sincerity in his eyes told me *this* was the real Cameron Fox. I got the impression Cam didn't let a lot of people in, which made it feel a little dangerous, knowing he'd opened that door just for me.

We walked in silence for a few steps, our hands still linked and our feet crunching over the fallen leaves. At the end of the path, we stopped at a stone ledge overlooking the lake, where Cameron gently pulled me against him, his hands resting on my waist.

To anyone passing by, we probably looked picture-perfect in our matching hoodies, stealing a kiss against the ledge. No one could see the way his hand crept up beneath my layers of clothing until his fingers found the curve of my breast. Nobody could hear what he whispered between kisses. "The sinful things I'd do if no one else was around..."

The wind carried his words away, and the moment was just ours. But while my body leaned into him, my head started to spin.

What were we doing? What *was* this? In a matter of weeks, this man would be far away from here, and I'd be stuck at The Underwood Hotel waiting for my life to make sense again. Wasn't this a little reckless?

Cameron must have been able to sense a shift in my mood, because he leaned slightly away, furrowing his brows. "You okay?"

I nodded, but it was followed by a deep sigh. "Sorry. I can't shut off my brain."

"What are you thinking about?"

"Should we have set some rules for what we're doing here?"

He gave me a lopsided smile. "You know what? I was just standing here thinking that nothin' gets me more aroused than some fuckin' *rules*." The last couple of words came out with a laugh.

At least he was taking my overthinking in stride. I giggled right along with him, shaking my head at myself for ruining the moment. "Okay. Now I realize how ridiculous it sounds."

"Nah. Not ridiculous." He pulled me in closer, breathing in through his nose as his hand traveled around to my back. "We can't exactly ignore the fact that I'm leaving once my contract is up."

I nodded, tracing the letter R on his hoodie with one finger. What if he was wrong? What if we *did* ignore the inevitable end? What if we didn't count down the days or label whatever this was trying to become?

Back in Chicago, I let myself get stuck in a relationship with a man who let me think what we had was forever. I'd spent so much time imagining a wedding when there was never even a ring, and I daydreamed about our life together like it was just about to begin. When it all came crashing down, I felt like I was the only one who hadn't seen it coming.

I'd spent so much time planning my future that I was never really focused on the *now*.

And maybe that was the difference. I didn't need a plan with Cameron. I didn't want to even think about what happened... *after*. It didn't matter.

What mattered was that I was here now, standing at the edge of the lake wearing this man's hoodie with the October breeze whipping through my hair. What mattered *now* was the worried look in those green eyes as he tried to figure me out.

"But what if we *did* ignore it?" I suggested, my voice sounding so small and uncertain. "Maybe that's our one rule: no discussing what happens after. We just let ourselves exist in this moment. Like November is never coming."

Cameron lifted a single, skeptical brow. "Are you proposing we just pretend November doesn't exist?"

"Exactly. November's not real."

He let out a quiet chuckle, his eyes catching mine with a playful glint. Would he indulge in this little fantasy with me? "November who? Never heard of her."

I hooked a finger on one of his belt loops, anchoring myself to him. "One might even say that people who believe in the existence of November are delusional conspiracy theorists."

Cameron's hands slid down my back until they reached the tops of my thighs, just below the curve of my butt. He grinned, pressing his forehead against mine. "Are you sure we're not the delusional ones in this scenario, Lucifer?"

"I never said we weren't." I tipped my chin upward, daring him to argue with me.

Cameron bent down and kissed me slowly, taking his time like he had nowhere else he needed to be. I let the comfort of his touch wrap around me like a blanket and pretended there wasn't a deadline looming over us. That this wasn't fleeting. And I sank into that beautiful delusion, letting myself believe we'd have October forever.

Chapter Thirteen

Cameron

AT NIGHT, WALKING DOWN the dim second-floor hallway felt like stepping through a haunted dollhouse. Lucy was waiting upstairs, but if I rounded the corner and a pair of creepy-ass identical twins asked me to come play with them, she was on her own for the night.

I turned into the little vestibule by the elevator and, thankfully, found only Virgil there—no ghost children in sight. He was carrying a drill and a piece of broken chair rail, and his face lit up in surprise when he saw me. "There's the hero of the day!"

"Hey, Virgil," I said, stretching my arm to hit the up arrow–and then, at the last second, I let my hand drop. What excuse did I have for going up? I rubbed my palm on my clean jeans, deciding I'd ride down to the lobby with him instead. Maybe I could grab a drink first, or something. "Who's been calling me a hero?"

"Well, the Wheelers, of course." The elevator doors opened, and we both stepped inside. We stood shoulder to shoulder, nearly the same height. "Said you relit the boiler. Thank you for handling it, but I should've been here for that."

"Well, it was late. You can't be here all the time, right?"

Virgil sighed and rubbed his forehead with the back of one hand, the other one clutching the drill and wood piece against his body. "They tried to get a hold of me, and I let them down."

Fuck. "Hey, you didn't let anyone down. I mean, look at how you've kept this place up and running for so long. I bet this building would fall apart without you."

That made the guy smile a little. "I've been here a long time. I think I know this place better than my own house."

The elevator doors opened, and I followed Virgil out. "What keeps you here?" I eyed the liver spots on his forehead. "You should be chilling on a beach in Florida or something."

I slowed my steps to match his pace as we turned toward the lobby. "I'm not much of a beachgoer," the old man said with a laugh. He ran his hand along the raised floral pattern in the wallpaper as we passed. "It wouldn't be easy for me to leave this place. I almost feel like this building's got a soul of its own sometimes. That probably sounds a little funny, doesn't it?"

Though I chuckled, I nodded like I understood. And in a way, I kind of did. This old hotel wasn't anything at all like the soulless, boxy buildings I'd constructed over the years. The Underwood had character. It had life.

I glanced over at Virgil. "No, I get it. And whenever you do retire, I bet this building is gonna miss you just as much as you miss it."

He let out a little snort of a laugh. "Maybe so," he said, nodding good-bye before ducking through a door that said EMPLOYEES ONLY.

I continued down the hall, heading straight for the bar. I got there just in time to hear the tail end of "Dream a Little Dream of Me," performed by the redhead who had been making Derek and the other dipshits on my crew lose their damn minds lately.

The bartender, wearing a paisley-patterned button-up shirt, gave me a double look as I approached. He flipped his phone over on the bar and leaned onto his hands. "Well, hi there. What can I get for you tonight?"

I spotted a chalkboard menu that listed some specials and quirky seasonal drinks, but that wasn't what I had in mind. "Someone recommended a beer that's exclusively brewed for the hotel... some kind of lager?"

"Room 313?"

"Yeah, that," I said, giving the lounge singer a polite smile as she sat down a couple barstools away, a cup of something icy already in her hand. Turning back to the bartender, I asked, "Do you have that in a bottle?"

"Yes, sir."

"Okay, gimme one of those, please, and... actually, make it two."

The guy raised both eyebrows as he turned around and pulled two bottles of Room 313 from the mini fridge on the back wall. "Are we really thirsty tonight?"

"One's for a friend," I explained, pulling out my wallet.

"A lady friend?"

The redhead in the barstool slapped the counter, almost spitting out her drink. "Ronnie! You can't just ask him if it's for a lady friend!"

The bartender scoffed and shrugged in innocence. "I'm sorry for being a little curious! I'm just making conversation with my customer!" He turned to me, accepting the money I handed to him. "Sorry for being nosey."

I chuckled. "No worries. And yeah, it's for a... lady friend."

Ronnie and the redhead exchanged looks as he opened the drawer for my change. He looked like he was holding his breath—or perhaps holding in another nosey question.

But it was the redhead who very quietly whispered, "Lucy?" The word was muffled by the cup in front of her lips, and I couldn't even be completely sure it was Lucy's name she'd said.

"What?"

Ronnie threw my change on the bartop and gave the redhead an incredulous look. "You did *not* just ask him if Lucy's his lady friend after chastising me for my way-less-invasive question. You're a nosier bitch than I am."

I picked up both beers with one hand, shaking my head with a grin. "Are you two friends of Lucy's?"

Ronnie's eyes danced with the realization that this all but confirmed I was on my way up to Lucy's room. "We are. But not in the way *you* apparently are."

"I didn't say a thing."

"Don't worry, Lucy will," the redhead said, giggling into her drink.

"C'mere," Ronnie said, motioning for me to get closer. I was confused until he reached across the bar and started rolling up one of flannel shirt sleeves. "Thank me later. Lucy's hot for your forearms."

I laughed, switching the beers to the opposite hand so he could roll up my other sleeve. I raised one eyebrow at the singer. "Is he always like this?"

"No. He's usually worse."

***

Ronnie was right about the forearm thing. My rolled-up sleeves were the first thing Lucy looked at when she answered the door wearing a silky pumpkin orange tank top and matching shorts. And then she saw the beers.

"Hey! You remembered!"

I handed her one as I entered the room. "Met your friends, by the way. They're... intense."

She twisted the cap off her bottle and tossed it on her dresser. "Sorry about them. Greta and Ronnie kind of have no filter."

"I picked up on that." I twisted off my bottle cap and dropped it onto the dresser beside hers, and we clinked our bottles together. I raised mine for a sip, a little surprised by the sweet apple taste. "Not bad."

"Right?" Lucy lowered herself to the foot of her bed, sipping her own beer as she pulled her legs up to sit cross-legged. Feeling less nervous than the night before, with something to hold in my hands, I sat next to her. The mattress dipped under our combined weight.

"I ran into Virgil a minute ago. Seems like he feels guilty for not being around last night to relight the boiler."

"Oh no," Lucy said with an exaggerated frown. "He doesn't need to feel bad about that. Everything worked out, thanks to you."

I looked down at my bottle. "I kinda feel like I stepped on his toes."

"I'm sure he doesn't think of it that way, Cam."

Every time that woman called me *Cam*, it sounded like she'd known me for years, like we were old friends. I took another sip before turning back to her, getting a better look at her silk pajamas that left little to the imagination.

I met her gaze again and held it. I thought about what Virgil said, about how hard it would be to leave this place–and then I remembered what Lucy said the night before about spending almost nine years away.

She must've left here the second she got the chance, and I was desperate to know why. Especially when she spoke so fondly of her childhood here. Something wasn't adding up.

"Virgil said this building has a soul," I said, glancing down to study the gothic details on my bottle's label. "Would you agree with that statement?"

She tilted her head to the side, giving it some consideration. I watched her eyes trail the floral wallpaper and intricate plasterwork on the ceiling. "I mean, it definitely feels like it has... life. This building knows all my secrets, that's for sure."

I cleared my throat, putting my hand just behind Lucy on the mattress. "Then you've got me dying to know why young Lucy Wheeler was so desperate to leave this place and not come back for nine years."

Lucy let out a soft sigh, reaching up to adjust the strap of her tank top. "You've met Janine Wheeler, right? Enough said."

"You and your mom didn't get along?"

"Not when I was eighteen. She hated everything I did. The boys I dated. The way I dressed. The music I liked. My late nights out. My tattoo. My friends."

"...Tattoo?"

She grinned at my curiosity, but she continued. "My mother thought everything I did was just for the sole purpose of pissing her off. It absolutely killed her that I didn't want to follow in her footsteps here. And when I graduated college, I was so desperate to prove I could make it in the city that I barely visited home."

"Too proud?"

"Yes. Until I had to come pathetically crawling back."

"No. Pathetic would be to struggle when you had this place to come home to." I lifted my beer to my mouth and took a generous sip, feeling Lucy's eyes on me the entire time.

"I'm glad I came here," she said, her voice low.

I swallowed a gulp of beer and faced her, picking up on the sudden tonal shift. "Me too."

Her lips lifted in a mischievous, teasing smile that made my pulse speed up. I could see the devil in her eyes just then, and nothing excited me more. "Where do you think my tattoo is, Cam?"

I smirked and leaned forward to set my bottle on the hardwood floor. "Well, let's see," I said, rubbing my palms together. It was time for a little scavenger hunt—one that I knew would have the most satisfying prize.

My gaze swept over her body, and I started with the knee closest to me. I ran my fingers down to her calf, lifting her ankle up onto my lap. I inspected every last inch of her soft leg, right down to her toes.

"Nothing on this leg. Give me your other one."

Lucy put her bottle down and followed instructions, bringing her other foot up to my lap on the bed. I repeated what I had just done, gliding my hand over her skin like I had all the time in the world, my fingertips trailing down the side of her calf to her ankle.

"You're very thorough," Lucy pointed out. I lightly tickled the bottom of her foot, making her throw her head back and laugh.

"I'm just getting started."

I gently nudged her feet off my lap so I could reach the rest of her body, starting with her waist. Tucking my hands beneath the silky fabric of the top, I slowly lifted it upwards with my wrists. Lucy raised her arms to allow me to pull the tank all the way up over head. I tossed the garment aside, holding my breath for a few seconds to appreciate the sight of her exposed skin. The soft curves of her breasts made my mouth ache to taste her, but I couldn't be that greedy. Not yet.

And so far, I hadn't seen any hint of a tattoo.

I touched her waist, trailing both hands up her sides, my fingers just brushing past the swell of her breasts. And then I pulled her close to me, her bare chest pressing against my body as I bunched her hair up in one hand to get a clear view of her back. My lips skimmed the curve where her neck met her shoulder while I searched for any hint of ink. Nothing there.

"Well, this game is getting more interesting," I murmured against her neck.

"I guess you're going to have to keep searching."

I eased her backward against the center of the mattress, and she sank down into the plush white bedspread beneath me. Lowering myself with her, I pressed a trail of kisses down her chest until my mouth closed over one nipple. She gasped and arched up into me, the sensitive point peaking under my tongue. *Fuck,* I didn't want to stop—but I couldn't let myself get too distracted. There was still a mystery tattoo to be found.

My right hand drifted down her body until it reached the waistband of her silk shorts. I gave them a tug, and Lucy lifted her hips just enough to help me ease them off, biting her lip in a desperate attempt to hold back a smile.

And there it was, a delicate rose outline inked into her skin, the top of it peeking out from beneath the thin band of her red panties. I let out a pleased chuckle as she kicked her shorts off her feet.

"So this is the scandalous tattoo that had Janine clutching her pearls," I said, running my fingers over the curvy lines of the flower. I lowered my mouth to kiss along her side, moving lower and lower until I pressed my lips against the ink just above her panties. With one hand, I hooked my thumb under the thin strap at her hip and tugged it down just enough to uncover the rest of the rose.

"It's so embarrassing," Lucy said, lifting her head to see me. "It doesn't even mean anything."

"But I like it," I said, and with both hands, I tugged her panties down to her thighs, revealing a part of her I wanted to get even more acquainted with. I gripped the red fabric and dragged it slowly down her legs, letting my fingers graze the side of her knees and ankles on the way down. When I finally tossed them onto the floor, Lucy was completely bare for me.

I braced myself over her again, lowering my mouth to the soft skin of her inner thigh. As my lips inched higher, I heard her breathing change, becoming more rapid and shallow.

How long had it been since I had a naked woman stretched out before me like this? I wasn't about to rush the experience. I took my time, inhaling the scent of her, enjoying the way her leg muscles tightened when I got closer and closer to where she wanted me. When my lips finally hovered above the apex of her thighs, I glanced up to see her watching me from behind her long eyelashes, her cheeks flushed.

Then I leaned in, letting my tongue slide against her in one long, slow stroke, knowing I'd never forget the sound that emitted from her when I tasted her for the first time. That soft, breathy moan hit me like a jolt straight to the core.

As my lips closed around her clit, her hips lifted against me, her feet pressing into my back in a desperate plea for more. With one hand curled around the back of her thigh, I slipped the other one between us, easing a finger inside of her as my tongue moved in slow, teasing circles.

"Goddamn, Lucy," I murmured against her, my breath brushing over her most sensitive spot. She buried her hands in my hair and gave my strands a gentle tug. "You taste too good."

I went deeper, flicking my tongue in sync with every slow curl of my fingers, building her higher with each stroke. Lucy's breathing turned ragged and her thighs tightened around my head. And then she let out a loud, broken cry, her legs trembling violently on either side of me. I felt her toes curl against my back and I kept going, letting her ride each wave while I tasted every last second of it.

When I pulled up to my knees, I watched Lucy's chest heave, smirking down at the complete mess I'd made of her. It took her a few seconds to catch her breath. And then, in one swift move, she rose up and shoved me flat against the mattress, taking control. I widened my eyes at the speed in which she clawed at my shirt to lift it away.

"Damn," I panted, struggling to hold myself up.

"You've done enough for me. It's your turn," she rushed out, pausing to reach up and touch my face with both hands. She lowered her mouth to mine for a quick kiss before leaning over to knock the rotary phone off her nightstand. "And I don't want any distractions."

I couldn't help but laugh—partly at the absurdity of her attacking her own phone, but mostly from the rush of realizing Lucy Wheeler was about to strip me bare. She hooked her fingers in the waistband of my jeans and underwear, dragging them down together.

Lucy knelt between my legs, her gaze fixed on me as her fingers curled around the base of my cock. She slowly ran her tongue up the length of me, making me forget how to breathe for a few seconds. And then she closed her lips around me, her mouth hot and wet, working in tandem with her hand in a way that had me wondering how I'd ever survive this woman.

"Fuck," I whispered, tilting my head back against the pillow. Before I could even get out another sound, Lucy pulled her mouth away and shifted forward, straddling me. She pressed her core against my length and began to grind.

"I'm sorry," she whispered, pressing her hands hard against my chest. "I really need you."

"Um. Don't apologize for that." I squeezed her hips, letting out a strained laugh.

"Could you wear a...?"

"Yeah,' I said, clearing my throat as I slid my hands down to her thighs. "I brought one. It's in my–"

There was no time to get the words out, because Lucy was already pulling a condom from her nightstand. And then she tore the foil open with her teeth and rolled the latex down over me with an efficiency that nearly made me lose it right there.

One of her hands braced on my chest, the other guiding me to her entrance. And then she sank down on me in one slow movement that made me breathless.

My head fell back against the pillow with a low groan, my eyes fluttering because *Jesus Christ*, nothing in the world had prepared me for how she'd feel. When I opened my eyes again, she was above me, her hair spilling forward and dangling over my face. I reached up in an attempt to move some of her hair out of the way, but it only slid out of my fingers.

Her palms pressed against my chest to steady herself, rocking her hips in a way that felt so good it made my vision blur. Every time she lifted herself a little just to take me all the way in again, I swore I could feel her tightening around me.

"Lucy," I whispered, gripping her hips to keep her close to me. She leaned down, catching my mouth with hers. Her moans vibrated against my lips, and I knew I wasn't going to last much longer if she kept this up. "You have no idea what you're doing to me."

Lucy pulled back enough to stare down into my eyes, her lips parting as she lowered herself onto me again, taking more of me inside of her. The sight of her like this, all flushed with her eyes glazing over with pleasure, was almost too much.

And then she whispered, "I can feel you stretching me out," and that was it. My body tensed as pleasure tore through me, drawing out an animalistic groan from deep within my chest. I sank my fingertips into

Lucy's thighs, squeezing her until the last wave of pleasure shuddered out of me. And the way she tightened around me, her body twitching like mine, told me she'd reached her second climax at the very same time.

"Oh God, Cameron," she breathed, letting out a sound that was a mixture of a gasp and a laugh as her body shuddered again. Still struggling to catch her breath, she eased off me and collapsed onto the pillow, letting me slip my arm under her head. "There," she said, pushing her sweaty hair away from her eyes. "We're even now."

I couldn't help but laugh. "Even? No. I still have that note. And I'm going to cash it in when you least expect it."

Her lips curled into a grin, and we lay like that for a moment or two–it was hard telling how many minutes passed, really, since I tended to lose my sense of time when I was with Lucy. I stroked her arm in silence, feeling grateful my job had led me here. To this.

She shifted in my arms, tilting her head up to look at me. "I really love just living in the moment with you."

I reached over to brush a strand of hair off her forehead and kissed her there. "You just read my mind."

Chapter Fourteen

Lucy

"Living in the moment" with Cameron made every day blur into the next. Some nights we were all tangled together between my sheets, neither of us knowing where I ended and he began. Other times, we just ordered room service in bed and watched low-budget horror movies, laughing at the horrible special effects until our cheeks hurt.

And honestly, those nights together were just as fun.

After a while, I suggested he start staying the night in my room, leaving his stuff there so he wouldn't have to slip back to his own room after midnight all the time. Cameron agreed without giving it a second thought, almost like he was relieved I'd asked.

In the daytime, we found little moments to sneak off to the conservatory or go for walks along the lakefront, where the leaves in Hathaway Park seemed to turn brighter shades of red and gold by the day. We knew our time together was limited, so we soaked up as much of each other as we could, letting every kiss and conversation linger.

And neither of us ever spoke of November, knowing it might break the spell we were under.

"Cold out there?" my dad asked as I stepped into the main office one afternoon, shrugging off my jacket to hang it on the hook behind the door. Both of my parents looked up from their desks, which faced each other at the center of the room.

Because nothing says *true love* like staring at your spouse's face all day long.

I raked my fingers through my hair, glancing at the painted portrait of nine-year-old me above the filing cabinet. With my pale skin and perfect posture, you would have thought I was just another one of the sad Victorian kids that adorned the rest of the walls—if not for my hot pink Mary Janes.

"Just a little breezy," I finally answered.

"How was your walk?" My mom stapled a few sheets of paper together and then flipped open a black binder. "Are you tracking your steps or something?"

I inhaled as I smoothed out my brown skirt. "No, I just like the fresh air. These walks help me clear my head."

"Did you notice the progress on the village?" my dad asked, interlocking his fingers behind his head. "They're ahead of schedule. The schoolhouse is already done."

I held back a smile. If only he knew I was getting a full progress report straight from the foreman's mouth every day, often while one of his hands slipped under my sweater. "Yes, I noticed. Those guys work fast."

My mom looked up at me from her binder. "Well, then let's not waste time. We need two or three antique school desks for the staging, and I'd like you to take the lead on sourcing them, Lucy. Check the antique stores in town tomorrow."

I nodded. My mom didn't hand responsibilities like that to me often, especially not a task with a budget attached. If she was letting me take the reins on this, it meant she believed I could actually pull it off. And I wanted to prove her right. "Sure, I can do that. Is there anything else I should look for?"

My dad pulled the hotel credit card out of his wallet. "Yeah, a deal. Don't be afraid to haggle with them. Especially on the delivery fee."

"Got it." I took the card and tucked it into my skirt pocket. Before I turned to leave, I caught my parents exchanging a quiet glance, both of their gazes drifting to that painting of me on the wall. And then, almost in unison, they returned to their work.

***

"I should have known that agreeing to shack up with a woman meant there'd be vanilla bubble baths in my future," Cameron said, his breath tickling the back of my neck.

I laughed, the sound echoing off the tiled walls as his arms tightened around my waist in my clawfoot tub. It was barely big enough for two people, but somehow we managed to wedge ourselves together. We'd just worked up a sweat in my bed, and this seemed like the perfect way to clean up. Together.

"Don't even try to pretend like this doesn't feel good after a long day," I said.

He kissed my shoulder. "It does. I needed this more than you know."

I turned my head to focus on his eyes. "What makes you say that? What's wrong?"

His face softened when he noticed my concern. "Nothing. My muscles just ache, that's all."

"Are you sure?"

He didn't immediately nod or tell me he was fine. Instead, his gaze dropped to the bubbles floating on the surface of the water. "Well, there is this one thing."

He paused to clear his throat, lazily moving the vanilla-scented bubbles around with one hand.

"At James's parent-teacher conference last night, the teacher gave me this drawing he did. And he... drew himself crying with these big tears coming down, and the teacher wrote on the bottom for him: *I feel sad because my dad has to move far away.*"

My hand flew to my mouth. "Oh!"

"I know. I damn near choked up in that classroom." His voice sounded rough like he might be about to choke up *now*. "The thought of having to leave Michigan for this next job is tearing me apart. For a lot of reasons."

His eyes found mine, and I didn't look away. "Maybe this is a dumb question, but do you absolutely have to take on this Tennessee project?"

Cameron nodded. "We've already committed to it. I'm not the only guy on the crew with a family. Derek doesn't even remember what his daughter looks like."

"That sounds like more of a Derek problem," I said with a laugh. I thought of what Cameron had told me about his recent weekend with James in Kalamazoo—and how he made him chocolate chip pancakes and strawberry milk. "James is so lucky to have you, Cam. Even when you're not physically present, you're showing up for him. He feels that love. I mean, he wouldn't have made that drawing if he didn't."

His lips parted, and for a few seconds, he just stared. Maybe he needed to hear he was a good father. Judging from the surprise in his eyes, this was the first time he'd considered things from this angle. "I guess you're right."

"I know I'm right."

"I'm starting to accept the fact that you're pretty much always right," he admitted with a laugh. His fingers teased my nipple just above the bubbles as he kissed the side of my head. He scooped up some water in his hand, letting it dribble down my chest. "I'm glad I don't work tomorrow. The guys would be wondering why I smell like a fuckin' cupcake."

"You'd be the best smelling guy out there. But hey, speaking of tomorrow." I adjusted my position, making the water shift and slosh from side to side. "I'm heading downtown to see if I can find a couple of antique school desks. I'd love to skip the delivery fee. If only I knew someone with a pick-up truck…"

He smirked. "Very subtle, Lucifer. I can take you."

"You'll go antiquing with me?" I asked, unable to hide the excitement in my voice. Smiling, I rested my head against him, my wet hair clinging to his chest.

"Yeah. I've barely ventured into Underwood. You can show me a little bit of the town, if you want."

On the inside, I was cheering, but I did my best to play it cool. "Yeah, we could eat at The Raven's Nest for lunch and make a day of it."

Cameron's right hand slid down my abdomen. "Did you say 'day' or 'date'?"

I stilled. "Which one do you think I said?"

"I don't know, that's why I'm askin'."

"Then which one do you *hope* I said?"

His fingertips drifted lower until his hand rested between my legs. As his lips brushed along my temple, his fingers began to move in slow, deliberate circles there. Finally, he answered, "Date."

My smile was so wide my cheeks hurt as Cameron teased my clit with featherlight strokes under the water. "Fine. It's a date."

"Good," he said, pressing his lips against my shoulder. My eyes drifted shut as he continued working me with his fingers, every stroke finding just the right spot. His left hand came up to rest against my neck, applying just enough pressure to make my pulse flutter against his fingers. "Should I keep going, or have you had enough tonight, baby girl?" he asked in that warm, husky voice that melted my insides.

Those words unlocked something within me I didn't even know existed. By day, I could run circles around people in this building and never lose control. But right now, I was Cameron Fox's *baby girl*—and I was about to come apart.

"Don't—"

I tried to choke out the words "don't stop," but that was as far as I got. My hips lifted and my back arched against Cameron's chest as the tension snapped. I gripped both of his forearms to steady myself, gasping against his neck until the very last wave of my orgasm shuddered through me.

Cameron was still smirking as he pulled his hand up out of the water and curled his fingers around the edge of the clawfoot tub. "Well," he said, holding me tight with his other arm. "I think we can retire *Lucifer* now. *Baby girl* suits you better."

Chapter Fifteen

Cameron

"Wow, look who can clean up."

Lucy grinned at the sight of me in the itchy, too-warm, beige sweater I'd purchased from the men's boutique in the hotel. Could she tell how uncomfortable I was wearing something besides a hoodie or flannel? "This sweater was fifty-seven dollars," I mumbled as we made our way down the hall toward the elevator.

"And worth every penny, right?"

I grunted in response, but I half-smiled anyway, wanting to tell her that yes—it was worth it for the way it made her face light up when she opened her door just a moment ago.

And it was the right choice, too, considering Lucy wore a dress that day and looked like an absolute knockout in it. Even as I scratched my neck beneath the collar of that fuzzy thing in the elevator, I was glad I hadn't worn one of my damn hoodies. I wouldn't look worthy of standing next to her. Probably still didn't.

"Are you worried one of your co-workers will see you with me?" Lucy asked when we stepped off the elevator.

"You kiddin'? I'm more worried about your mom seeing you with me. She'll ream my ass."

Lucy grinned. "I thought you said my mom loves you."

"Doesn't mean she wants me messing around with her daughter."

That made her laugh as we stepped off the elevator, the smell of coffee and maple syrup drifting from the bistro area. We wove our way through guests checking out or heading back to their rooms after breakfast.

The sun was bright that morning, but there was a chill in the air. As we approached my banged-up blue truck in the middle of a row of luxury sedans and shiny SUVs, I swallowed.

"I, uh... I had a nicer truck, but I sold it a while ago," I explained, reaching for my keys in my pocket. "I wanted something practical I could throw tools in and haul stuff without worrying about the paint job. So just, you know, I'm sorry about the way it looks."

Lucy tucked a soft curl behind her ear as she looked up at me. "Oh no, a hard-working man who uses a truck for its intended purpose? What a complete turnoff."

With that, my insecurities dissipated into thin air.

I opened her door for her, shaking my head at the playful way she rolled her eyes. I'd only taken two steps toward my side of the truck when something hit me like a sucker punch to the gut. I knew, in that moment, that walking away from this woman on the first of November was going to destroy me. I'd gotten so used to her and the way she could sling my sarcasm right back at me that the very thought of leaving it all behind made me feel almost hollow inside.

But when I climbed into the driver's seat, I pushed that all aside. We'd made a rule to never speak of what happened when October ended, after all, and I wouldn't let any mention of it ruin our day.

Our *date*.

***

Underwood, Michigan sure loved its ghost stories. Of course, I'd already heard about the lady in the lighthouse, who was sometimes seen pacing the observation deck, waiting for her lover lost at sea. But as we walked down Main Street, Lucy rattled off the other local legends. An old theater haunted by a vaudeville performer. A candy store cursed by its original owner. It seemed like every storefront we passed had a story.

And Lucy knew them all.

"Honestly, I'm convinced they all invented a ghost story just to attract customers," she admitted, "but can you blame them?"

I nodded, squeezing her hand as we neared the first antique store. "Are there ghosts at The Underwood?"

"I mean, yeah, a lot of people have died in that building, Cam. The spirits that haunt our rooms are actually real."

She said it with casual certainty, as if she were blissfully unaware of the double-standard. But when she turned to nudge the antique store door open with her hip, she paused to wink.

"You're so full of shit," I muttered, following her through the red door which led us into, fittingly, Red Door Antiques. The place smelled like dust and was stuffed wall to wall with old furniture and shelves of vintage toys. We walked from room to room, keeping our eyes peeled for an antique school desk or two, but we didn't have any luck. Lucy walked out with a 1920s-era art deco brooch, though, and she seemed pretty satisfied with herself.

Our next stop was Lakeshore Treasures, and after that, I followed Lucy around a thrift store that sold more clothing than anything else. I could tell she was getting discouraged as we walked away empty-hand-ed. And then, after Underwood's fourth and final antique store led to another disappointment, the crinkle between her brows was hard not to notice.

"Hey," I said, glancing at the time on my phone as I closed the door to Underwood Curiosities behind us. I ducked beneath a cluster of dried corn stalks around the door frame to join Lucy on the sidewalk. "It's about lunchtime. What do you say we head down to that place you were tellin' me about, grab a bite to eat, and then work on a plan?"

She stuck her hands in the pockets of her wool jacket and took a deep breath. "Okay. I just really thought we would've found something by now."

"I know." I touched her lower back as we curved around a skeleton seated on a rocking chair on the sidewalk. Someone had propped an old book in its lap and stuck reading glasses on its nose. "Let's figure it out after we get some food in you."

That earned me a small, grudging smile. "Are you trying to imply I'm hangry?"

"I said no such thing."

Lucy huffed, but she didn't argue, and we made our way toward the restaurant down the street.

Either The Raven's Nest was already decorated for the season, or this was how it looked year-round. Black candles in brass holders crowded the hostess stand near the front, and stuffed ravens were posed in all the stone alcoves. The decor reminded me a little of The Underwood Hotel, to be honest, and it made sense that Lucy suggested this place. The host led us toward a booth in the back, where a stained glass window made the place feel more like an old chapel than a café.

After the server took our orders, I leaned onto my arms and watched Lucy tilt her head back to study the details in the stained glass. She smoothed her windblown hair with both hands, and when her eyes finally caught mine, she gave me that little half-smirk that always wrecked me.

It suddenly occurred to me that I was on an actual date with an actual woman–the first one in many, many months. I had a few dates right after the divorce was finalized, but they didn't really feel... right. They didn't feel like *this*. They didn't make my chest ache in this weird way, like I was getting too close to something I never wanted to lose.

I tapped my fingers on the table. "You look like you belong in a place like this."

"What's that supposed to mean? Do you think I'm creepy?" She lifted one eyebrow at me.

I chuckled, fidgeting with my straw wrapper. "No. I mean you've got that classic Hollywood beauty. Like you could've stepped out of a black and white movie and no one would question it."

Her smile softened, and for a second, she didn't say anything—she just looked at me like she wasn't sure what to do with that kind of compliment. Then she tucked a strand of hair behind her ear and said, "Just wait until you see my Halloween costume."

"Oh, now I'm intrigued."

She tilted her head. "What about you, are you dressing up?"

"Nah."

"Come on. What if James asks you to?"

I took a deep breath, and though I shook my head, I knew that if James asked me to wear a costume, I'd cave in a heartbeat. It wasn't like I hadn't before. "Maybe. We went as *Wizard of Oz* characters when he was two. I was the tin man, and he was the scarecrow. His mom went as Dorothy."

She crinkled her nose with a cute laugh. "That sounds really cute."

I shrugged, even though the memory made me smile. I could still see James toddling around, refusing to keep his hat on while Vanessa and I walked him down the streets of our neighborhood.

Across from me, Lucy's expression shifted as she focused on my eyes. "I've been curious about something," she said, stirring her drink with her straw. "But it feels kind of nosy to ask."

She didn't have to.

"You want to know what happened with me and James's mom," I stated, catching the sheepish smile she tried to hide.

I settled back against the cushiony booth to get more comfortable, trying to decide whether I should water it down or give her the full story. Part of me hated talking about this, but I had nothing to hide and no reason to keep any of it from Lucy.

"I thought Vanessa and I were doing okay, but I was away a lot," I said, running one thumb down the side of my glass. "One Friday, I got rained out on the job and came home for the weekend earlier than she was expecting. And when I opened the garage door, this other guy's truck was there."

Lucy gasped, and I just nodded to validate the reaction.

"One of her co-workers. I walked in and found them in bed together."

"Oh my God. What did you do?"

"Turned right around and walked back out. I didn't stick around to hear her excuses. Picked James up from daycare and took him with me to my mom's house for the night. And Vanessa... she tried to say it was my fault for being away too much."

My leg shook up and down beneath the table. I hadn't said any of this out loud in a long time. And, perhaps sensing my discomfort, Lucy reached across the table to rest her hand on my wrist. "I'm so sorry, Cam. You didn't deserve any of that."

I let out a slow breath to ease some of the tightness in my chest. "Well, life's messy sometimes. And James makes it all worth it."

Before she could respond, the waitress appeared with two bowls of soup and pretzel rolls to share. We both thanked her before unwrapping our spoons and diving in.

"God, I've missed soup," Lucy said in a dreamy voice as she stirred hers.

"Did it.. go away?"

She laughed, holding her spoon up to her mouth. "No, asshole. I just mean that other than microwaved Campbell's chicken-and-noodle in my hotel room, I haven't had any decent soup in a while. It puts me in a fall mood."

I tore off a piece of warm, buttery pretzel bread and took a bite with a nod, grateful to be spending this day in Underwood with the incredible woman in front of me. It was a sharp contrast to how I spent my first couple of Saturdays in this town, rotting in my bed alone.

"So," I said, dipping my bread in my loaded potato soup. "What's the plan for today? You seemed pretty distraught about not finding the desks."

"I just don't want to call my mom and tell her I came up empty," she said, sighing as she glanced down at her butternut squash soup. "Sometimes I feel like she still sees me as that irresponsible eighteen-year-old girl who left home and had no idea what she was doing. I need her to know she can trust me."

"How're we gonna prove Janine wrong, then? You can't just give up after four stores."

"There aren't any others in Underwood, and I can't expect you to drive me all over Michigan searching for these desks. I might try eBay, but then again, the shipping costs..."

I let my spoon rest on the edge of the bowl and leaned onto my arms again. "The shipping would be outrageous. Let's just keep searching.

You navigate, I'll drive, and we'll keep going until we find what we're looking for."

"You don't want to do that," she said with an awkward laugh.

With a self-assured grin, I leaned in close enough that the people at the next table wouldn't hear me say, "Don't tell me what I do or don't want to do, baby girl."

Lucy tried not to smile, but her cheeks turned the slightest shade of pink. "Fine. I'll let you take me. But we have to do something you want to do, too. What would make this your perfect day?"

Was she serious? It already was.

But I knew she'd want an actual answer, so I picked up my spoon to eat a couple more bites, giving it some thought. "I think," I started, mulling it over in my mind.

What did I *really* want to do with Lucy?

"I think we should get a bottle of whiskey and sit on the beach after dark."

Lucy's mouth fell open. "But it'll be cold!"

Though she protested, she couldn't help but smile. With a shrug, I grabbed another pretzel roll and tore off a little piece as I met her eyes across the table. "I'll keep you warm."

Chapter Sixteen

Lucy

Lord Huron drifted from the speakers as Cameron's truck rambled down the highway, and I couldn't help but watch the way his forearm flexed every time he shifted gears. He took his hand off the wheel for a few seconds to scratch his elbow. Even with his rolled-up sleeves, I could tell that sweater was irritating him. It was all I could do not to laugh.

The road ran parallel to Lake Michigan, giving us glimpses of the water here and there between patches of trees. The fall foliage was at its peak, with bursts of red and gold lining both sides of the road. It was the kind of beauty that made me grateful to call Michigan my home.

I checked the map on my phone, counting down the miles until we hit Saugatuck and its cluster of antique shops. As I zoomed in on the town in the app, something to the right caught my eye outside the car.

Up ahead stood a weathered pink building with a massive wooden ANTIQUES sign nailed across the front. With its steep gabled roofs and a tall tower in the center, it looked like it could've been a church at one time.

"Stop here," I blurted. Even if they didn't have any school desks, I was dying to meet the kind of person bold enough to paint an old church bubblegum pink.

Gravel crunched under the truck tires as Cameron pulled into the lot. Up close, the place looked even more eccentric, with a collection of windchimes dangling from the eaves and dead vines crawling up an old wooden ladder that looked like it had been forgotten decades ago. A faded, hand-painted *Cleo's Antiques* sign was nailed to the pink siding beside the door.

The inside smelled like mothballs and wood polish. Floorboards creaked in the next room, followed by the voice of an older woman shouting, "Welcome in! If you need anything, just shout!"

The small front room of the place was cluttered with shelves bowing beneath the weight of old books and kitschy collectibles. Cameron wandered toward a display of Mackinac Island souvenir plates with his hands tucked in his pockets, and then he froze when his eyes locked on something in the next room.

He blinked a few times, and then he just said one word. "Oh."

"What is it?"

I stepped around an elegant steamer trunk to get a better look through the narrow doorway, bracing myself for something bizarre or unsettling. We'd seen our share of unusual items that day—Cam said the collection of clown figurines at Underwood Curiosities would haunt him for a while.

What was he looking at now?

And then I saw them.

Three old school desks, the kind with cast iron legs and a bench-style wooden seat attached to the front. They were identical, and with them lined up in a neat little row, I could already picture them sitting inside our haunted schoolhouse. I walked over to the first one and lifted the price tag. $150 felt like a steal—but then again, I didn't know much about pricing antique furniture.

Cameron followed me into the room, running his hands over the glossy wood on one of the desktops. He eyed the cracked porcelain doll in the seat, her glassy eyes staring straight ahead like she was waiting for class to begin. There were two other dolls seated at the other desks, too, their expressions just as eerie.

"If they come with the creepy-ass dolls, do we have to take them?" Cameron asked, turning away from the doll with one closed eye like he didn't fully trust it.

I held back a grin, amused by what could make this grown man squirm. "But Cameron, Mildred needs a little dolly to play with."

"Mildred needs an exorcism," he deadpanned.

I laughed and motioned for him to inch out of the way so I could snap a picture for my mom, who'd probably question why I'd brought Cameron Fox with me. I knew I'd eventually have to explain how I got the desks to the hotel, but I wasn't ready for that conversation.

Her reply came almost instantly—a thumbs up emoji and a follow-up text that said: *Get all 3.*

It wasn't exactly gushing praise, but a thumbs-up from Janine was like a standing ovation. I'd take that.

"Can I help you two with anything?" A thin, silver-haired woman wearing cat-eye glasses and three or four bracelets on each wrist emerged from a smaller room in the back. "All furniture is ten percent off until the first of November."

"Perfect! I'd like to get all three of these desks, then," I said, nodding toward them. And then, without meeting Cameron's eye, I said, "And I just love that doll there, the one with the blonde curls? Could you possibly throw her in with the sale?"

The woman, who I assumed was probably Cleo, lit up with a smile. "Yes, I can absolutely do that for you!" She clasped her hands together, making her bracelets jangle like the windchimes outside. "I can't tell you how thrilled I am for these desks to have found a new home. They've been sitting here for ages. And so has little miss Sally."

I finally looked at Cameron, who was trying to smile politely but looked like he might be suppressing a scream. I had to bite the insides of my cheeks so I wouldn't giggle at the murderous glint in his eyes.

"Sally?" I asked, turning back to Cleo.

"Oh yes, I give all the dolls names. Sometimes they're the only company I keep around here. Anyway," she said, picking up the creepy doll before yanking the price tag off one of the desks. "Come on up to the register."

Cleo walked into the next room, but before we followed, I turned to give Cameron a sly grin.

He shook his head. "You know that doll's probably possessed, right?"

"She'll be right at home at The Underwood, then," I said, glancing over my shoulder at Cleo, who was wrapping the doll in tissue paper behind the register. And then, lowering my voice to a whisper, I turned back to Cameron and said, "That woman is everything I aspire to be when I'm older."

He blinked at me a couple of times, holding back a smile. "I knew I should've run when you got excited about the corpse flower. That was my first red flag."

I just laughed, accepting his outstretched hand as we walked toward the front.

Cleo offered to call her son to help Cameron load the desks into the truck, but Cam brushed her off and handled it himself, carrying each one like it weighed nothing. He refused to let me pitch in, so all I could do was stand back and hold the door for him.

"Hang onto that one," Cleo murmured to me after he carried the last desk past us. I was confused until I realized she was talking about Cameron. "Strong hands and gentle eyes are a good combo. Reminds me of my second husband. He was my favorite."

I just nodded, unsure it was appropriate to giggle at that last remark.

Back in the truck, I got myself situated and quickly buckled Sally into the middle seat while Cameron tightened the straps around the desks to make sure they wouldn't budge. And when he came to the driver's side and opened the door, all I could do was grin at him over the top of the doll's stiff blonde curls.

"We're ready," I said.

He froze, one hand on the door handle and the other on the metal frame of the truck. "You know what, Lucifer? You're lucky I like whatever's wrong with you," he said with a grunt as he slid into his seat.

I burst out laughing, the sound filling the cab as he started the truck and shook his head. And then he leaned across the seat to steal a quick kiss, his hand gripping my upper arm like he was afraid I'd slip away. When he pulled back, his eyes lingered on mine, almost unreadable, and I couldn't help wonder if I was starting to mean something to him.

Neither of us said a word.

Sally sat buckled between us, looking equal parts prim and unnerving, as the truck pulled away from the pink church. And when I looked over at Cameron, he was quietly smiling to himself. I tucked my hair behind my ears, turning my gaze toward the trees whizzing by as we passed.

Hold onto that one.

If there were a way to hold Cameron in place and make him stay forever, I'd do it in a heartbeat.

***

"Out of all the things you could've chosen for your 'perfect day', this is what you wanted to do?" I passed the bottle of apple bourbon back to Cameron and pulled the blanket tighter around me. I'd brought one to spread out across the sand beneath our butts and another to wrap around our shoulders. They helped, but it was Cameron's body heat against my side that did more to keep me warm from the breeze rolling off the water. The lakefront was dark, with only a sliver of a crescent moon above us and a dim light from Hathaway Park in the distance.

Cameron just shrugged as he took a sip and then pulled the bottle away, touching his mouth with the back of his hand. "Because I knew we'd have the beach to ourselves. And it's just... ours."

He wasn't wrong. We'd been sitting there for ten minutes, and I hadn't seen a single soul. Probably because nobody in their right mind would be on the beach at this time of night, this late in October. But there we were, huddled together like a couple of lovedrunk idiots.

"We can go back inside if you're cold," Cameron said, tightening his grip around my waist.

"No, I'm fine." The second the words rolled off my lips, my whole body gave away the truth with a shiver. I laughed at the knowing look Cameron shot me, cocking his head to the side. "Okay, I'm a *little* chilly, but I'm also cozy sitting here with you. I'm exactly where I want to be right now."

He was quiet for a moment, with only the sound of the waves filling the silence. He offered the whiskey bottle to me again, and when I shook my head, he screwed the lid back on and set it down on the blanket in between us. "Well. Fine. But if you change your mind, you'd better tell me."

"I will, I promise." I shifted my weight on the blanket so I was leaning into him more. Cameron kissed the top of my head and I closed my eyes. For a few minutes, we sat just like that.

If I could freeze any moment in time, this would be the one.

I almost said it out loud, but I drew my lips closed at the last second. Saying those words would come too close to that forbidden topic, that our time together was just temporary and, in November, we wouldn't have this anymore.

Instead, I rested my chin on his shoulder and wondered aloud, "How many days until James gets to come here?"

"Thirteen," he answered without even needing a second to count. "Vanessa's bringing him down that Friday evening so he'll get the full weekend here. And then on Sunday we'll..."

He paused, swallowing, and reached up to loosen the neck of his hoodie.

"...leave together," he finished. I noticed his jaw flex, but he hurried on before I could react. "I think I'll take him by the old train depot that morning. He's definitely going to want to see it himself after looking at that book from you."

"I bet he'll love that."

"Yeah," he said, finally turning back to look at me, a smile tugging at his lips. "But you know what else I'm lookin' forward to that weekend?"

"What?"

"Finding out what your Halloween costume is. You're being very secretive about it, which makes me curious."

I laughed, knowing my costume was so niche he was either going to be wildly impressed or deeply disappointed. "You'll just have to wait and see," I teased, brushing a bit of sand off the blanket.

"It's the devil, isn't it?" he guessed, reaching over to give my thigh a squeeze. His fingers roamed slowly up and down the buttery-soft fabric of my thick tights like he was really enjoying the way they felt.

He leaned in, closing the gap between us until his mouth found mine, sending a warmth all the way through me. We kissed between those two blankets until everything else faded away—the waves, the chilly October air, and every last thought in my mind.

When his hand skimmed up my side, I curled my fingers into the front of his hoodie and tugged, pulling him down with me until my back sank into the blanket beneath us. Cameron followed without hesitation, bracing himself over me as he kissed me even harder.

He pulled his face away from mine to glance up and around the dark beach. And then, his eyes returning to mine, he whispered, "God, I want you right here. Right fucking now."

I reached up to cup his face with both hands. "I'm not going to stop you."

Cameron lowered his mouth to kiss me, but just before his lips touched mine, he said, "But I didn't bring anything."

I lifted my hips, grinding against the hard length of him, needing him closer. "Neither did I, but I can worry about that in the morning. All I want right now is you."

I knew how desperate I sounded.

And I knew how reckless this was.

I probably should've cared more, but with Cameron's hard body pressed against me and his breath hot against my ear, all I could think about was how badly I needed him. Maybe it was because I knew our time was running out and the thought of wasting even one second on restraint felt unbearable.

Whatever the reason, I wanted him now, on this beach, between these blankets.

Cameron's hands scrambled at the hem of my dress, tugging it upward to push it out of the way. He hooked his thumbs under my tights and yanked them down, his touch rough and urgent. As the fabric dragged down my thighs in one hard pull, I gasped and laughed at the same time, helping him shove them lower until they bunched around my boots.

"Fuck, I might've ripped 'em," he said, pressing a kiss on the inside of one knee. "I'm sorry."

"Don't be sorry–keep going."

He fumbled with my underwear and pulled them down too, pausing to pull the blanket over our bodies. He dragged his lips against my neck, moving slow like he thought we had all the time in the world. But I didn't want slowness. Not tonight. I didn't want foreplay or teasing kisses or gentle touches.

I just needed to be filled by every inch of him.

My hands found his belt, unbuckling it with shaky fingers. I shoved his jeans and underwear down until he let out a surprised laugh against my throat. "Jesus, Lucy."

"We don't have much time," I rushed out.

I meant tonight.

Now, on this beach.

But when his eyes locked on mine, I knew he heard the other meaning too. The one we weren't allowed say out loud. His gaze lingered on me like he wanted to answer, but instead he leaned down for a quick and messy kiss.

With my fingers tangled in his hair, Cameron slowly pushed into me until I was gasping against his open mouth. The weight of his body pressed me deeper into the blanket against the sand, and suddenly, the chill in the air was the last thing on my mind. Cameron's forehead dropped to mine, his breath shuddering as he pulled back and sank into me again and again. Slowly at first, and then faster and harder until every thrust had me clinging tighter to him and moaning against his neck.

"God, I love feeling you wrapped around me," he rasped.

His words made me feel as good as the motion of his hips grinding against mine. I curled my fingers around the back of his head to drag him down for another kiss.

Cameron slowed down again, closing his eyes like holding back was the only way to make this last. Yet even in that slow rhythm, every thrust pulled me closer and closer to the edge without sending me all the way over. The blanket felt like a cocoon around us, hiding our dirty act from anyone who happened to be taking a walk up at Hathaway Park above the shoreline.

When Cameron stuck one hand under my knee to force my legs farther apart, the new angle forced a sharp cry from my mouth. I clenched tight around him, pleasure crashing through me in waves as my nails dug into his shoulders. My eyes flew open to find his already focused on mine just as the climax split me apart.

"Fuck," Cameron grunted, his thrusts becoming rougher. He buried himself deep in me until he lost control, too, and his release spilled inside of me.

For a moment, neither of us moved. We just clung together under that blanket, our chests heaving in sync. The only sound was the waves crashing on the lake and our ragged breaths.

And then, stupidly, I blurted, "I wish you didn't have to go."

My whispered words just hung there between us, getting heavier by the second. Cameron didn't agree–in fact, he said nothing at all as he rolled off me and yanked up his pants. The sudden absence of his body left me shivering as the blanket pulled away from my shoulders.

But my cheeks felt warm. Not from the sex–but because his silence as he lay on the blanket next to me was the loudest thing I'd ever heard.

We'd made one simple rule, and I'd just broken it without warning. I took this somewhere it was never meant to go. Cameron and I didn't talk about emotions and romantic feelings. Not like that. I'd just asked him for something impossible. Something he could never give me. Something he might not have even wanted to give me in the first place.

Why would he? He had the ideal situation here: a woman he could sleep with for a few weeks with no strings attached and no expectations. It was perfect.

And I'd just ruined it.

While I lay there spiraling, Cam shifted beside me. Without a word, he used one corner of the blanket to clean up the mess between my legs. Slowly and delicately, he pulled my panties and tights back up, the complete opposite of how he'd yanked them off. And then he lay beside me again, lacing his fingers with mine in between our bodies.

That at least reminded me he wasn't gone yet.

Chapter Seventeen

Cameron

By the start of the next week, we'd made some major headway on the haunted doctor's office and mortuary. I had some guys hanging drywall while others started painting. And with the haunted schoolhouse finished at the very end of the row, it was getting easier for me to visualize the complete project. The crooked, quirky little village was finally taking shape.

"We're almost there," I told the crew as we gathered around my truck for a water break. "I can tell you guys are pickin' up the pace lately. Keep it up."

Derek lowered his water bottle from his mouth. "Holy shit. Are my ears deceiving me, or was that praise?"

Wesley gave an enthusiastic nod, leaning against the side of the truck with his arms folded. "I think it was. What's got you in a good mood, boss?"

"My crew's finally getting their shit together. That's what."

"Hmm. Thought maybe there was something else," Wesley said with a doubtful stare. He knew *exactly* what was going on. Every time Lucy and I snuck off during lunch, I'd come back to find Wesley smirking like he knew where I'd been.

I didn't get the chance to tell him to shove it because Mrs. Wheeler approached from the garden, zipping an expensive-looking black jacket as she glided toward us. Some of the guys scattered and got back to work like they'd been caught slacking, but she didn't scare me.

In fact, judging from the way her face lit up when she saw the progress on the village, she was in a good mood. "Wow, this is really coming together. Right on schedule, too."

"Of course," I said, brushing my hands together as I walked up to her. "The doctor's office should be ready for staging as soon as the paint dries."

"Very nice, very nice." She crossed her arms and nodded her head, her eyes trailing down the entire length of the village. "You really know your stuff. Where did you learn all of this? Have you always been in construction?"

I shifted my weight on my feet. "Yeah, I learned a lot from my dad. He was a teacher, but he had a handyman business on the side. I tagged along with him to his jobs and picked up some skills that way."

"Did you go to trade school, then?"

"Yeah," I said, pausing to clear my throat. Why did I feel like I was at an interview? "I, uh, did a vocational program in high school, and then a carpentry program in Grand Rapids."

"Do you have family nearby?"

For a second I wondered why she cared, but I tried to keep my face neutral. "I have a son in Kalamazoo. He's four."

"Oh, I didn't know you had a son." Janine smiled, holding my gaze. "Is it hard to work this far from him?"

"Well, no. It's actually ideal for our custody agreement. My other projects usually take me much farther away. The next job I've got lined up is going to keep me from seeing him for weeks."

Janine just stared for a moment, like she was working something out in her head. Suddenly, it hit me that this wasn't casual small talk–she was interrogating me for a reason. She was *testing* me.

And in the back of my mind, I worried she'd somehow figured out I'd been dating her daughter. She knew I'd been the one to load the desks into my truck on Saturday, and no matter how casual Lucy tried to play it, I had a feeling Janine was too sharp not to read between the lines.

Was she trying to make sure I was good enough?

Man enough?

Her next question didn't help. "Do you ever see yourself finding something more stable instead of traveling all over the place?"

I reached up to rub the back of my neck, glancing over at the crew carrying sheets of drywall toward the haunted bank. God, how I wished I were over there with them instead of getting the third degree from Lucy's mom. "Maybe, one day. Depends on what it is."

Janine nodded like she was taking mental notes, and then she took a couple backwards steps away. "Well, I won't keep you. I just wanted the chance to get to know you a little better, Mr. Fox."

We said goodbye, and as I returned to my work, all I could think about was how Mrs. Wheeler was only wasting her time trying to get to know me. Because in eleven days, this was over. This job. My stay at The Underwood. This... thing with her daughter. All of it.

I was just there to build a damn haunted village and move on. That was it.

At the back of the mortuary, Derek was showing Holden a loud video on his phone, both of them cackling like it was the funniest thing they'd ever seen.

"Stop fuckin' around," I muttered in their direction as I picked up my drill. "We've got less than two weeks to finish this job. Come on now."

Derek slid his phone in his back pocket and put his work gloves on. I caught him mumbling about me when he got back to work. "That good mood of his sure didn't last long."

***

I trudged up the brick path toward the hotel with my head hanging low, my lunchbox strap digging into my shoulder. The day had been long, and Janine Wheeler's little interrogation hadn't done my mood any favors. I was already counting the days left in Underwood, but that interaction only served as a reminder that I couldn't build anything long-term with anyone.

And maybe Lucy and I had already gotten too close. As I trailed behind my crew through the rose garden, I kept replaying the way she'd said she wished I didn't have to go—and how I hadn't been able to say anything back. I just froze like a fucking idiot.

She wanted more than I'd ever be able to give her.

There were moments when I considered suggesting trying something long-distance, but I knew that whenever I came back to Michigan, my first priority had to be James. I wouldn't be able to juggle being a good father and a good boyfriend when my visits were going to be so short.

Lucy deserved someone who could give her everything, and that sure as hell couldn't be me.

Up ahead, Virgil caught my eye as he climbed down from a ladder next to one of the wrought-iron lampposts at the edge of the walkway. The rest of the guys walked past him without a word, but I slowed down when I got close. He leaned against the ladder with a paint can in one hand, his breathing loud and uneven in the quiet garden.

"You going to call it a day, Virgil?" It was after five, and I figured the old man's wife was probably waiting for him to come home.

He didn't laugh or reply at all. Instead, his face scrunched into a grimace, and he braced himself harder against the ladder.

I stopped on the walkway, resting my arm on my lunchbox. A flicker of dread stirred in my gut. "You alright?"

Virgil shook his head, lowering the paint can to the ground before easing himself down beside it. Once he was seated on the grass, he reached up to press the heel of one hand against the center of his chest, his breaths becoming even more shallow. "Got a phone on you, son?"

"Yeah, do you need to call someone?" I answered, immediately fishing for it in my back pocket.

Virgil took another loud, sharp breath. "Call 911," he panted. "I believe I'm having a heart attack."

Chapter Eighteen

Lucy

By the next evening, I'd put myself in charge of collecting signatures for Virgil's *Get Well Soon* card, hunting everyone down like it was my only job. I found Marie folding stacks of white towels in the laundry room. After my parents and me, she was the next to sign, tearing up as she wrote Virgil a little message.

"I can't imagine this place without him," she said. "Your mom and dad used to always say he came with the building, you know. He even knew the Hathaways before they passed on."

"I know. Virgil's kind of the glue that holds the foundation of this place together."

"That's exactly right." Marie snapped the cap back on the pen, and I continued making my rounds, taking the card to the kitchen crew, the concierge, Ronnie and Greta, and every other member of the staff who knew Virgil.

Which was, essentially, everyone in the entire building.

Marci at the reception desk was my final stop. She signed her name with swoopy letters, topping the *i* with a star. "So what happened?" she asked, lowering her voice so the guests seated in the couch in the lobby wouldn't overhear. "I know he had a mild heart attack, but nobody's told me the details."

"You know the construction guy, Cameron? The tall, blonde one with the broad shoulders and the...?" My voice trailed off as Marci nodded, smiling like she knew exactly who I was talking about—and what was making me ramble like that.

It was no secret Cameron was an attractive man, but I probably could have done a better job of hiding my lust for him. I reached up to fidget with the ends of my hair, feeling heat creep up my neck.

"Anyway, he was the one with Virgil in the garden when it happened. He called 911 and sat with him until the ambulance got there, and then he followed it to the hospital. He stayed with Virgil until Rosemarie got there."

"Aw. And I bet Rosemarie was a complete wreck. She's always coming in here telling him he works too hard or that he needs to come home for supper."

I grinned as I tucked the card under the flap of the envelope—I still had one more signature I needed to get. "Cam said she ensured he was going to be okay and then proceeded to chew him out for having the audacity to almost die."

Marci laughed. "See, that's the kind of love I want. Or a love like your parents', at least."

"My parents?"

She pulled a strand of blue-green hair away from her eyes to get a better look at me. "Um, yeah. Their office door is ten feet away. They're either in there bickering or being disgustingly lovey-dovey."

That sounded pretty accurate. My parents had been married for more than thirty years, and even when they clashed over hotel nonsense, it was never the kind of thing that left scars. They always worked things out.

Right on cue, the office door swung open and my parents stepped out hand in hand, both of them looking tired at the end of the long day. My mom gave my dad's hand three squeezes before strolling up to the desk.

I spoke before she did. "Hey, I'm going to take the card and gift basket to Virgil up at the hospital in a little bit."

"He's not there," my mom answered as she reached for the mail on the back counter.

My stomach lurched. "He's not there? What do you mean?" For one horrible second, I assumed the worst.

My mom must've read the panic on my face, because she rushed on, the corners of her eyes crinkling with a gentle smile. "Relax. He was discharged this afternoon. Rosemarie said he yanked out his tubes and told the nurses he was going home."

Of course he did.

"I'm sure he had to sign some papers acknowledging he was going against medical advice," my dad said, shaking his head. "But that's our Virgil. Stubborn as heck."

My mom sighed as she used a long fingernail to slice open an envelope. "Sadly, I think that was the wake-up call he might have needed. It's time for him to retire before his body makes that decision for him."

For once, I couldn't disagree with her on that.

My dad nodded as he reached up to adjust his wire-rimmed glasses. "Funny, I always thought we'd be passing Virgil on to the next owners."

Those last two words made my breath catch in my throat, sending a sharp ache to the center of my chest. *Next owners.* He'd said them without even a second of hesitation, like it'd already been decided.

"The next owners?"

He just let out a casual laugh, shooting my mom a quick side glance as he stood with his hands on his hips. "Well, sweetheart, your mom and I aren't getting any younger. We'll have to think about selling eventually, especially since, you know, you haven't shown much interest in taking over."

I opened my mouth to say something, but only a squeak came out. The thought of someone else owning The Underwood Hotel had never occurred to me. Not once. To imagine driving past it one day and having no connection to it was unthinkable.

Because to me, this place was more than just a building.

It was just like Virgil told Cameron: The Underwood had a soul. Letting it go would feel just like losing a loved one. I knew every creaky floorboard, every chandelier, and every secret hiding spot. This hotel had practically *raised* me.

At one end of the counter, Marci checked in some late-arriving guests, and my parents carried on talking about a few maintenance issues that would need attention soon. And I just stood there holding Virgil's card against my chest, grappling with the horrifying thought of some stranger holding the keys to this place.

A few minutes later, the sight of Cameron pushing through the revolving door jolted me right out of my spiraling thoughts. He strolled across the lobby toward us, a paint can in one hand, a paintbrush in the other. My heart gave a little kick when he shot a quick subtle grin in my direction before walking straight up to my mom's end of the reception desk.

"Mrs. Wheeler," he said, putting the paint can and brush down on the counter. He smiled at my mom like they were old buddies. "You're gonna wring my neck."

My mom crossed her arms, but my god, her eyes sparkled when she looked at him. "What did you do, Mr. Fox?"

Cameron sighed, glancing down at the paint can. "I took it upon myself to pick up where Virgil left off the other night, and I touched up the last couple of lampposts in the garden. This stuff was just sitting out, anyway, where any of the guests could have grabbed it."

I'd always heard people talk about feeling weak in the knees, but that evening in the lobby, I felt it. My legs went so wobbly I had to lower myself to one of the chairs behind the desk, pressing the Get Well Soon card against my chest like it might calm my fluttering heart.

Cameron had no idea how devastatingly attractive he was to me in that moment.

My mom put one hand on her hip like she was prepared to scold him. "And let me guess, you're going to refuse to let us compensate you for the labor, aren't you?"

"You already know."

My dad stepped forward, his hands folded behind his back. "Well, we certainly appreciate the extra help. You're a good person to have around in times of crisis, it seems."

Cameron's eyes dropped to the counter. He just gave a little nod, clearly struggling to accept the compliment. "It's nothing."

A moment later, my mom slipped her arm under my dad's and turned to me. "We're going to call it a night, Luce. Let's drop off the basket and card at Virgil and Rosemarie's tomorrow. I'll go with you."

"Okay."

She gave me a quick kiss on the cheek before tugging my dad toward the revolving door. He adjusted his glasses, telling me goodnight before offering Cameron a polite nod of approval. And then they were gone.

I exhaled and looked up at Cam, who was still leaning against the desk, smirking down at me without a clue how hard I was falling in that moment. Not only had he been there for Virgil, he'd made my mom smile and earned my dad's respect. Without even trying.

This man was just supposed to be a grumpy, human space heater delivering nightly orgasms. What business did he have making me swoon like this?

I stood up and glanced over at Marci. "Hey, can you keep a secret?"

She looked up from her phone and nodded, one brow lifting with curiosity. "Yes?"

Before I could overthink it, I leaned over the counter and kissed Cameron on the lips. For a beat, he froze, and then he was laughing against my mouth.

"You really are the devil," he whispered before kissing me back, both of us ignoring Marci's stifled giggles at the other end of the desk. And then Cameron pulled slightly away, just enough to stare into my eyes.

"Okay," Marci said, her hand half-covering her mouth, "when you said you had a secret, I assumed you had gossip. Not whatever *that* was."

Cameron chuckled at her before his eyes drifted back to me. "Actually, I'm not sure it's a secret anymore."

"What?"

"Your mom was interrogating me the other day, almost like she was seeing how I measure up as a man. I think she's got us figured out."

I used to be better at hiding things from my mother, but maybe I was slipping. Had she noticed the way I couldn't look her in the eyes when I said Cameron casually offered up his truck? She could probably guess why my voice softened every time I mentioned his name, and it was just as likely she knew who I'd been taking my midday walks with.

I rested my forearms on top of the card on the desk. "Well, do you think you passed Janine's test?"

"With flying colors."

For a moment, we held each other's gaze across the reception desk, and the rest of the lobby faded into the background. I barely even registered the guests Marci assisted at the other end of the counter. I wondered if Cameron and I were thinking the same thing–that it didn't matter what my mom thought of him or this relationship, anyway.

We were in the single digits now, getting closer and closer to that inevitable goodbye. And yet, in moments like this, it was hard not to imagine more.

I forced myself to tear my eyes away, glancing down at the card as I pulled a pen from my skirt pocket. "Hey, will you sign this for Virgil?"

"Of course." He took the pen and twirled it between his fingers before clicking it against the counter. "Any more updates on the old man?"

"Well, considering he yanked out his tubes and busted out of the place, I'd say he's on the mend."

Cameron let out a husky chuckle as he signed the card. "Why am I not surprised? He's one tough old bastard. I get the feeling he'll insist on coming back in here tomorrow like nothing happened."

"I don't think my mom will let him. I'm actually almost positive they're going to force him into retirement after this."

He clicked the pen against the counter again and slid the card back toward me, his knuckles brushing against my arm. "As much as I hate to say this," he said, his tone unexpectedly gentle, "that's probably the right decision at this point."

I slipped the card into the envelope, tucking the flap inside while trying to swallow the lump in my throat. Between the situation with Virgil and my dad casually mentioning the prospect of new owners, it felt like the ground beneath me was shifting. And if I let myself think about Cameron leaving too, the weight of it all was almost unbearable.

Cameron's eyes softened as he watched me. "Hey," he said quietly. I lifted my eyes to his. "It's not like Virgil's disappearing. He's left his mark on this place. I mean, you can see it everywhere you look."

I let out a breath, glancing at the polished wood beams above us and the patchwork of mismatched tiles on the lobby floor. "Maybe that's why it feels like this building has a soul," I said, pressing my palms flat against the counter. "Because it carries a little bit of everyone who's ever come and gone. It's like they all left pieces of themselves behind, and somehow the building remembers."

Cam pointed at me. "There's the writer in you coming out. I hope I read about this in the next Underwood newsletter."

I wrinkled my nose with a snicker. "You don't read our newsletter."

"Like hell I don't. Where else would I learn about the Hathaways transforming this building from a seminary dorm into a luxury hotel a century ago?"

Damn, he really had read it, and he had the receipts to prove it. The smug little curve of his smile, like he knew he'd impressed me, made me swoon for the hundredth time. And with our time together rapidly running out, I knew I was just asking for heartbreak.

Chapter Nineteen

Cameron

There were thirty-two ornate plaster tiles on the ceiling of Lucy's room. I'd counted them twice–once a couple nights ago, when I couldn't sleep, and again this morning, when my alarm went off and I couldn't bring myself to get out of bed. Next, I found myself counting Lucy's heartbeats against my side, reaching a hundred before I told myself I needed to get up.

Four was the number I couldn't shake that morning.

Four days until James arrived.

Four mornings left to wake up with Lucy's arm heavy across my chest. It was like I was counting down to the best and worst day of my life at the same time.

We weren't talking about it. I was sure she had a countdown in her head, too, and knew that this had to end when James arrived. So much was left unsaid, but I could read it in her eyes when we kissed goodbye in the mornings.

For the past few days, she'd been scheduling room service to deliver breakfast for the two of us. This happened after I confessed my first meal of the day usually consisted of an energy drink and a protein bar. Lucy didn't like that, so she made a deal with the kitchen to send us a daily tray with eggs, bacon, fruit, and the most buttery croissants I'd ever eaten.

I grumbled about it at first, pretending I didn't like being fussed over. But the truth was, it kind of did something to me. The gesture made me feel cared for in a way I didn't realize I'd been missing. And hell, if I didn't secretly look forward to that knock every morning.

Tennessee would be so lonely.

My alarm didn't wake Lucy, and neither did the noises I made as I shuffled around the room to get ready. I would have thought the knock at the door would've jolted her awake, but it wasn't until I brought the tray of food to the bed that she opened her eyes and sat up almost immediately.

"Surprise, surprise. The smell of bacon finally wakes you from your slumber," I teased, removing the polished silver covers from each of our plates.

Lucy grinned, wiping the sleep from one eye with her fingertips. "It's not the bacon. It's the cinnamon rolls."

She nodded toward the two styrofoam containers at the edge of the tray. "Is that what I smell?" I settled in beside her on the bed, crossing my legs as I picked up my fork. "I don't know if I'll have room for that, too."

Lucy scooted closer to the tray. "Then take it with you and have it at lunch."

For a moment, I was silent while I ate, watching Lucy add an ungodly amount of salt and pepper to her eggs. She'd told me a couple mornings ago it masked the "eggy" taste and wouldn't accept my suggestion that maybe she didn't actually like eggs at all. Our pseudo-argument ended with her rolling her eyes and me laughing like I'd won.

"I still don't think I deserve all this," I said, waving a hand over the whole spread. "Especially because you won't let me pay."

"Shut up and let me feed you, Cam."

The intricate pattern on the edge of my plate held my focus. I wasn't used to being somebody's priority. Half the time I didn't think I'd earned the right to be.

"But I'm just some... guy," I murmured.

Her fork hovered in front of her mouth. "Yeah. *My* guy. Eat up."

I brought my eyes up to hers, letting the words hang there. She paused, too, lowering her fork to her plate with an unreadable expression. We both knew I couldn't be her guy—not for much longer, anyway. And yet, every so often, we allowed ourselves to slip so comfortably into this thing between us, it was like it had no expiration date.

Then there were moments like this, when neither of us could ignore how our mornings together were fleeting.

"You're so bossy," I said, in an attempt to ease the awkwardness. In the back of my mind, I knew we'd have to face our truth by the end of the week, but I wasn't ready for that conversation right now. It could wait.

Lucy's lips curved upward. "Just admit you like it when I tell you what to do."

I just huffed out a laugh, stabbing another bite of eggs on my plate. She had no idea.

***

The Wheelers hired a set designer from the local community theater to finish staging the haunted village and pull everything together in the final week. Between her, her crew, and the actors rehearsing their jump scares, it turned the last week of construction into pure chaos.

We were nearly finished, installing doors and shutters and adding molding to the interior of the last two little buildings. We worked as harmoniously as we could with the other crews, keeping out of their way and thanking them for keeping out of ours, but they were distracting my guys.

"Not that I'm complaining," Derek muttered around the nail he was holding in his teeth, "but if that woman bends over in front of me again, I'm gonna forget which end of the hammer to use."

The young set designer was bent over an antique rug at the edge of the garden, adding fake blood splotches with a spray bottle. This was apparently too much for Derek and a couple of the other guys, who needed twice as long to hang a set of shutters they should've had up in ten minutes.

I decided to let it go. It was after five, and we'd gotten enough done for one day. I was anxious to see Lucy, anyway. Every minute counted.

"Let's just pack it up for the night before you go and hurt yourself," I mumbled, before yelling toward the rest of the crew to call it a day. The late October air felt cold on my cheeks as I made my way up the walk toward the hotel. I wondered what winter in Tennessee would feel like. Would I even see snow?

"Mr. Fox." The second I pushed through the revolving door, Janine came around to the front of the reception desk like she'd just been waiting to pounce. "I'd love to chat with you about something. Is now a good time?"

There was something eerily suspicious in Mrs. Wheeler's smile. As ready as I was to get upstairs and take a shower, I found myself nodding and following her into her office. Curious. And, for the first time, a little scared of her.

The walls in the Wheelers' office were lined with dark wood paneling, and at the center sat two desks pushed together back-to-back. Above the filing cabinet hung another painting of a little girl. But unlike the gloomy

Victorian children staring down from the other rooms in this place, this one actually looked cheerful. In fact...

"Is that Lucy?"

Mrs. Wheeler lowered herself into one of the desk chairs, motioning for me to sit in a leather chair nearby. "What gave it away, the pink shoes she refused to take off for her portrait sitting, or the mischievous look in her eyes?"

It was the latter–that and the beauty mark by the corner of her mouth. But I didn't say any of that out loud. Wasn't sure I could without grinning so hard I'd give myself away. Instead, I just chuckled as I sat down. "Just had a feeling."

Janine gazed across the room at the painting. "I still see that little girl when I look at her sometimes. I blinked and she was grown. I'm sure that's something you're starting to understand with your little boy, isn't it?"

I shifted my feet on the rug, afraid I was dirtying it and the chair I was sitting on with my filthy work clothes. But she was the one who'd asked me in here, and she didn't seem to mind. "Don't remind me. I think he looks bigger every time I see him."

She tilted back in her desk chair and crossed her arms against her chest. "How often is that?"

It couldn't be more obvious she was sizing me up. Trying to figure me out because she knew I'd been messing around with her daughter.

Fuck, this was a million times worse than picking up a girl for a date in high school while her dad polished his shotgun in the living room. As sweet as Janine sounded, there was still something about her unwavering gaze that made me feel like I was on trial.

"Every other weekend," I answered. "That changes sometimes, depending on my needs or his mom's. Like, for example, we shifted things around this month so he could come for Halloween."

That made Mrs. Wheeler tilt her head to the side. "Your son is coming this weekend?"

"Yeah." I relaxed my shoulders, grinning at the thought of James seeing everything we'd built and all the Halloween decor going up around the lobby. "I didn't want him to miss it. He's going to love this place."

Her expression softened, and for a second I thought maybe I'd imagined the whole interrogation vibe. "That's wonderful," she said, almost to herself. Then she straightened, folding her hands on the desk. "Mr. Fox, I'll get straight to the point: I'd like to try to steal you away."

I blinked. "Come again?"

"I've been watching the way you work. You take initiative, and you lead well. And you've jumped in without hesitation in times of crisis. That's the kind of person The Underwood needs. I'm asking you to consider becoming our permanent groundskeeper, stepping into Virgil's role."

For a second, all I could do was stare. I'd braced myself for questions about Lucy, not a job offer. "Groundskeeper?"

"Yes." Mrs. Wheeler opened a manilla folder and slid a sheet of paper across the desk. "The salary is competitive, and the benefits are good—we take care of our people here. There are also groundskeeper quarters on the first floor with a kitchenette and private entrance. It's used for storage now, but it's where Virgil lived before he married Rosemarie."

My throat went dry.

She was offering me a steady job. A place to live. A reasonable commute to my son. A salary I could live with, especially if this meant room and board would be included. All of it was laid out on a single sheet of paper before me like Janine was daring me to turn it down.

It was then that I realized she didn't know I'd been messing around with her daughter. And if she had even the slightest clue, she probably wouldn't have made this offer. At least, not without running it past Lucy. She thought she was hiring a reliable man to keep the hotel running, not the guy who'd been slipping into her daughter's room each night.

"I..." I knew Mrs. Wheeler was waiting for an answer from me, but I didn't have one. The prospect of settling down in one place was always a distant dream, something I didn't think would come along for someone like me. Maybe not until retirement.

I couldn't remember the last time I'd stayed in a place for longer than a season.

"I understand it's a big decision," Janine said, locking eyes with me again. "All the worthwhile ones come with risks. You don't have to decide right away. But you should know..."

She leaned closer, as if making sure I was paying close attention.

"I've already spoken with Virgil about this. When I mentioned you stepping in, he seemed... relieved. Like he could finally rest knowing the hotel would be in capable hands after him."

Fuck.

That dryness in my throat turned into a lump I couldn't swallow. "Wow, I don't know what to say."

"I didn't tell you that as an attempt to manipulate you, just so you're aware," she rushed out. "I just thought you'd like to hear that. The decision is yours to make, but we would love to add you to the Underwood family."

James's drawing flashed before my eyes, the one he'd made at preschool, with tears flowing from a stick figure. And then a memory of Lucy on the beach came to me just as vividly: *"I wish you didn't have to go."*

But my father always told me that if something seems too good to be true, it probably was. *"There's always a catch,"* he would say.

And in this case, the catch was obvious. By tying myself to this hotel, I was tying myself down to Lucy and to a future I wasn't even sure she wanted with me. Never once had we discussed our feelings, something that felt like it was against the rules.

Janine didn't know what she was asking me to commit to.

"I'm just–" I stopped, dragging a palm down my jaw as I looked over the paper in front of me, listing all the duties of the job. "I'm not sure it's that simple. I mean, I love this place. The Underwood already feels like a home to me."

My eyes drifted toward the portrait of Lucy on the wall, but I wouldn't let them linger for more than a few seconds. I cleared my throat, focusing on a white splotch of paint on my jeans.

"I've committed to going down to Murfreesboro a week after I leave here. I'm not even sure I could get out of it this soon, to be honest."

I was making excuses. Rogers would replace me in a heartbeat without giving it a second thought. It'd make a few people angry, but they could get over it.

Janine nodded, the crinkles in the corners of her eyes becoming more prominent when she smiled. "I understand. It's a major life shift, so I'm not asking you to make up your mind right away. Take some time to really think it over."

I nodded, folding the paper she'd given me before sticking it in the pocket of my lunchbox on the floor next to the chair. "Thank you for even considering me."

Janine stood up, smoothing the back of her slacks as she came around her desk to walk me to the door. "I've always believed people end up in the right places at the right times. Call it serendipity, if you will. But if I'm wrong about that this time, then I'm wrong," she said with a shrug, resting her hand on the doorknob. "No hard feelings.

I managed a faint smile as I walked through the open door. "Thanks. I'll let you know what I decide."

"Have a good evening, Cameron."

My footsteps sounded heavy as I made my way toward the elevators, past the row of portraits of the building's former owners. I caught myself holding my breath when I reached the spot in the hall where Lucy and I shared our first kiss.

This was her place. It was her family's legacy, not mine. What business did I have to insert myself here, permanently? We'd barely scratched the surface of who we were to each other. As much as I'd grown to care about her over the last few weeks, I knew I had to be realistic.

I needed to consider everything. Every messy "what-if" and all the ways this could go wrong. Would a fight with me make Lucy's life more difficult? What if we broke up? She'd wake up every morning knowing she'd have to pass me in the hall, see me in the garden, or call me to come fix something.

Committing to this job meant forcing Lucy to commit to *me*, in a way. And that scared the hell out of me.

Chapter Twenty

Cameron

THE UNDERWOOD HOTEL HAD never felt more alive than it did on the Thursday night before Halloween weekend. The place was fully booked, according to Lucy, and the lounge overflowed with people looking to have a good time. Haunted house actors crowded the bar fresh off their dress rehearsal. Even more people trickled in from downtown after a long day of setting up rides and booths for the festival.

My crew only had a half day left on the schedule tomorrow, with most of them checking out by afternoon. They weren't planning to stay for Halloweenfest, like me. It was their last night together for a while, which they all saw as an excuse to get drunk.

"One night of fun won't kill you," Wesley had told me when I tried to say I wouldn't be joining them. And I wouldn't have, if not for Lucy's encouragement. We both knew this was our last night together, but that didn't mean we had to spend it hiding away in her room while a party raged downstairs.

So we joined the chaos, almost presenting ourselves as a couple–which barely made anyone bat an eye. Somehow, it was like they already knew.

But none of them knew there was a chance I might be staying at The Underwood for good. Fuck, Lucy didn't even know. Over the last couple of days, it became obvious Janine hadn't told Lucy about the offer, and

I didn't want to bring it up until I was certain of my answer. If I didn't decide to stay, there was no reason to weigh Lucy down with it.

Without saying it out loud, we both seemed to reach an agreement to treat tonight like it wasn't our last together. She didn't bring it up, and because my future plans were uncertain, neither did I. We just got swept up in the Halloween drunkfest at the bar and acted like nothing was ending at all.

With a full band behind her, Greta performed a sultry rendition of "Season of the Witch," and half my crew tripped over themselves like they'd never seen a woman before.

"She's raking in the tips tonight," Ronnie said, sliding two beers across the bar. "And that high slit in her dress is doing half the work."

Lucy glanced over her shoulder before turning back to us. "Greta's left thigh is paying her rent for next month."

"She looks like she's having fun with it," I noted, laughing against the rim of my beer bottle at the way Greta slid her dress up a little higher, dragging a long red fingernail across her skin. The guys in the front row were practically salivating. "She's got them all under a spell."

"I wish I had half her confidence," Lucy said, slipping her hand beneath my arm.

I swallowed a gulp of beer and cocked my head to the side as we inched through the crowd. "I don't know, I've seen you be that confident... just in a different way."

"When?"

Smirking, I remembered the way Lucy tapped that state senator on the shoulder to put him in his place. And then my mind flashed to the day we met in the garden. "How about when you yelled at me about that goddamn mechanical spider when you didn't even know my name?"

She scoffed. "I didn't *yell* at you."

"Like hell you didn't. I was shaking in my boots." I slid one arm around her waist to tug her closer. All around us, zombies with smeared blood bumped elbows with construction guys, still in their work boots. There was hardly any room to move side to side in that lounge, and almost no one was sober.

Over the course of the night, Lucy laughed louder with every drink. By her fourth, she was clinging to the front of my flannel shirt like she needed me to hold her steady. And that I did, along with trying–and failing–to guess what her costume would be that weekend. She refused to give me a single hint, other than to say that I might not "get it."

"I'm going to pretend you're not insulting my pop culture knowledge," I said, pulling her even tighter against me. I was glad her parents were gone for the night so they wouldn't witness the way her hands slid into my back pockets.

"It has nothing to do with pop culture."

"Then what the hell is it?"

"Just wait until Saturday," she said, laughing against my mouth. I went in for a kiss, tasting the alcohol on her lips and wanting nothing more than to take her upstairs for the night.

I only pulled away when someone tapped me on the shoulder. It was Greta, of all people, sliding in close as she placed a hand on each of our backs. "Cameron, I need you to give me all the tea on Wesley."

"Wesley?" I blinked at her.

"Yeah," she said, speaking low as she reached up to push her red, wavy hair away from her eyes. "There's a chance I'll go up to his room tonight when this is over. Tell me if I'm safe with him or if that's a big mistake."

I grinned over her head at Wesley, who was sitting in one of the leather loveseats with Derek and the other guys, keeping one eye on us. "Do you want the truth?"

Greta stared back with wide, nervous eyes. "Yes. Please."

"If I had to pick one guy from my crew for you to trust, it'd be him. Wesley's solid. A real gentleman, as far as I know."

I could practically feel her sigh of relief. "Oh, thank God."

"Get it, girl," Lucy said, pinching Greta's side. "And tell Ronnie and me all about it."

"Obviously." Greta winked at her before slipping away. She returned to the microphone to perform "Criminal" by Fiona Apple, which had all the other men in there ready to propose on the spot. Lucy and I watched Wesley hold a beer on his lap, trying to play it cool like he didn't notice Greta was singing directly to him.

The crowded bar area filled up with even more people, many of them spilling in from outside like they'd come straight from the Halloweenfest set-up. In the midst of everything, Lucy put down her empty beer bottle and fanned herself with both hands.

"You okay?"

"I need a little air."

I grabbed her by the hand and led her through the sea of bodies to the open lobby, stopping beneath the oversized wrought iron chandelier. "It's a little cold, but do you want to step outside?" I asked her.

"This is fine. There were just too many people in there." Lucy bunched her hair up at the back of her neck, gazing back into the lounge, where the band slowed things down and Greta began a haunting cover of "Stand By Me." A few people in the crowd coupled up, still holding their drinks in their hands as they embraced.

It was impossible not to notice Lucy's frown or the crease between her brows as she watched her friend sing through the crowd. I had the sudden urge to smooth it out with my thumb, but I thought of a different way to make it disappear. At least I hoped.

"Dance with me," I said, squeezing her hand.

Lucy's eyes darted from the couples swaying in the lounge to Marci over at the desk before landing on my face. "Right here?"

Without answering, I drew her in closer, lifting both of her hands to my shoulders. She looked like she might laugh at the absurdity of it or even pull away in embarrassment. Maybe this was too much.

Thankfully, when I wrapped my arms around her waist, the corners of her lips lifted and that crease between her brows started to ease. We swayed beneath the chandelier, its dim glow catching in her hair as she rested her head against me.

I closed my eyes like that might help me memorize the feel of every curve of her body and the sweet smell of her shampoo. Everything about her had become so familiar and safe and comfortable to me over the last month that the thought of never holding her again made my stomach drop. I felt like I was free-falling even though both feet were on the ground, leading Lucy in a slow circle on that cracked marble tile.

I pulled back so I could see her face, bringing one hand to her chin to tilt it upward. Her lips parted and then pressed together again, with confusion etched all over her face. I couldn't hold it in anymore—fuck our agreement. I needed her to know I couldn't stand the thought of only spending a single month with her. It wasn't enough. It never would be.

"Lucy." I swallowed. "November's just–"

"Don't," she interrupted, dropping her hands from my shoulders to my arms like she needed to put some distance between us. "Please don't say it."

"But we should–"

"We've made it the entire month without going there. It's almost over now and if you say what I think you're going to say, then it's only going to be harder. So please... don't. We had a deal, Cam."

Her words came out rushed, like she was desperate to cut me off before I made things worse.

My jaw clenched shut. She didn't even know what I was going to say, just that she didn't want to hear it. And maybe that was the answer I needed. Because if she was this afraid of talking about feelings, maybe I really didn't want to know what hers were.

Instead of pushing her, I conceded. "Okay." I rubbed my palms on the back of my jeans. "Then are you ready to go back in there, or do you want to go upstairs?"

"Upstairs."

I just nodded. If Lucy wanted to avoid words, I could give her that. I took her by the hand and led her down the hall, onto the elevator, and toward her room, trying not to read into every sigh and shoulder-sag.

Inside her room, we still didn't talk. I said what I wanted without words, slowly removing each article of her clothing, one by one, before nudging her toward the bed. All the things we avoided admitting came out in the way I touched Lucy's skin and tasted her, knowing this could be my last opportunity to ever be this close.

When I finally hovered above her body and pushed inside of her, she closed her eyes, and I begged her in my mind: *look at me. Just look at me.* And when she did, there were tears shining in her eyelashes.

I lowered myself to press a kiss to her forehead as we moved together, trying to tell her with every inch of me just how I felt, while searching for any sign she felt the same. She framed my face with her hands, and I pressed a kiss to her wrist before guiding one palm to my chest. I wanted her to feel my heartbeat against her skin as I sank into her again and again.

I clung to the way she cried out my name when she came apart beneath me, like it was proof she didn't want this to end.

After, when I held her, I almost said the words I'd been burying under the surface. I considered laying everything out about this job offer from her mom and how leaving her was tearing me apart from the inside–but I chose instead to honor her one request.

Besides, I still had a decision to make. And until I knew my answer, maybe I didn't need to risk putting that added weight on Lucy's shoulders. Especially if she'd made up her mind that this was over.

So I just kissed the top of her head, listening to her breathing slow down as she fell asleep in my arms. I'd give her tonight, like she requested. But I knew that before the weekend was over, we'd either be saying goodbye for good or agreeing to a long future together. There could be no in-between.

That night, I barely slept at all.

Chapter Twenty-One

Lucy

By lunchtime on Friday, the entire town was already alive with Halloween chaos. The festival was just hours away, launching with a parade down Lakefront Avenue. It was such a big deal in Underwood that the local schools released early.

Yes, really.

The haunted village was all set for its launch that night, with all the scare actors currently wandering the grounds for photo ops with guests. The construction crew only needed half a day to make some adjustments after their run-through the night before.

Inside the hotel, my mom and I split the work between us. We fielded questions from guests, handed out maps of the festival grounds with an attached itinerary of our hotel's activities, and juggled dozens of tiny crises that never seemed to stop coming.

On the outside, I probably looked like I had it together. I did my best to pretend like I wasn't unraveling. My hands shook as I re-strung the bat garland in the lobby, just feet away from the spot where Cameron held me the night before. Just the memory of the way he smelled as we danced beneath the chandelier nearly knocked me off the chair I stood on.

We hadn't officially said goodbye, knowing we'd see each other around the hotel all weekend. But when we parted that morning, there was a finality in our kiss like we both understood it was probably our last one.

Part of me expected Cameron to push back when I insisted we not talk about our relationship ending. But he was so quiet, it was like he'd already checked out. From here. From us. That was what gutted me the most—the way he honored my request so easily, like that was what he wanted, too. That morning, there were times he couldn't even bring himself to meet my gaze, and it was all I could think about.

"It's still not even, Lucy," my mom said, peering up at the bat garland with her hands on her hips. "The left side is sagging."

On any other day, I'd have some snarky response for my mom about her impossible standards or how she could hang these bats herself. I might have even muttered under my breath that she could shove them up her ass.

Instead, I quietly adjusted the garland to her liking and stepped down without even rolling my eyes. I'd call that personal growth.

When I returned the chair to the bar area, Ronnie motioned for me to come over. "First of all, look at you, Miss Pumpkin Spice," he said, eyeing me up and down as I walked over in my new orange-brown pinafore apron dress that I almost didn't wear that day. "I love this outfit on you."

"Thanks, Ronnie." I sighed, sliding my palms down the soft fabric.

"Why are you so gloomy?" He looked confused for a moment, but then he gasped. "Oh, your guy's taking off today, isn't he?"

"He leaves Sunday. But can we... not talk about that? Why did you wave me over here?"

He made a sad face, but thankfully, he let it go. "Fine. Have you talked to Greta?"

"Not yet. I wonder if anything happened with Wesley."

Ronnie smiled from one side of his mouth. "Oh, it happened. And he tried to extend his stay, but there aren't any rooms, so she's letting him shack up with her so they can fuck all weekend, I guess."

I slapped the bar. This was just the gossip I needed to distract me. "Are you serious?"

"Dead serious. She literally just texted about it. Says she's in love."

I crinkled up my nose and snorted. "She always says that."

Ronnie shook his head as he picked up a rag to wipe down the bar. "Are you sure you don't want to talk about your situation?"

"I'm sure. I need to get back to—"

I couldn't even finish my sentence before my mom's voice rang out from the lobby. "There you are, Lucy. I need your help with the kids' table. Let's hurry."

She disappeared around the corner without waiting for a response. No *"when you have time"* or *"when you're done with your conversation."*

I turned back to Ronnie, my shoulders slumping. "Remind me to schedule a vacation over next Halloween."

He arched one eyebrow at me. "Oh? You think you'll be around here next Halloween?"

The words hit a little harder than they should have. Without even realizing it, at some point I'd stopped picturing myself moving back to Chicago. I drew in a breath, giving Ronnie a little shrug as I stepped away from the bar. "We'll see."

My mother and I spent the next hour preparing the pumpkin painting area at the base of the twin staircases. We spread kraft paper onto two long tables, setting up rows of little pumpkins and acrylic paint sets.

She bent over the cardboard box I'd just stuck on the floor at the end of one table, pulling out a small white pumpkin with a scowl. "Where did all of these come from? I didn't think we budgeted for that many."

"Oh, they're left over from the Garza wedding last weekend," I said, pausing to open a package of stencils with my teeth. "Their wedding planner tried to throw them out, but I snagged them from the trash."

Her face softened, and she set the pumpkin back in the box with an approving nod before moving along the tables, spacing the chairs out evenly. "That was very resourceful of you. I think you get that from your dad."

"Probably," I said, forcing out a laugh even though I wasn't really in the mood. I thought for a moment, and then I added, "I'm never really sure if I'm doing a good job here."

My mom froze, her hands gripping the back of one of the folding chairs. "Of course you are. What makes you think you're not?"

"Well, I mean, I was thrown into this and given a million things to juggle, but you never really give me any feedback unless I've done something wrong."

She held one hand against the center of her chest. "You've just always been so independent and headstrong, I guess I wasn't aware you needed that validation."

"Of course I do. Doesn't everyone? Ever since I've been back, I've been trying to prove to you I can handle this job."

She came around the table, reaching up to smooth my hair off my shoulders like she used to when I was little. "Sweetie, you don't need to prove anything. I knew all along how capable you were. I rest easy every night knowing you're here. That you're safe. That I get to work with you. And that this hotel is in good hands."

Oh. That was everything I'd been needing to hear from her, yet I could think of nothing to say in response.

She squeezed my shoulders. "Okay?"

I nodded, and she wrapped her arms around me in a tight hug. For a moment, I let myself sink into it, inhaling her familiar perfume, the same powdery rose scent she'd worn for the past twenty years.

She had no idea how badly I needed to be mothered, not managed. And perhaps if we were just a little closer, I could tell her what was really on my mind that day. The words were on the tip of my tongue, but I swallowed them.

Maybe I'd tell her after he was gone.

"Speaking of this place being in good hands," she said when we slipped out of the hug. "Did your father mention we asked Cameron Fox to take over as groundskeeper?"

All at once, my blood ran hot through my veins and my stomach lurched. I held the back of a chair with one hand to steady myself, relieved my mom was turned away as she opened another package of stencils.

"No," I managed to say, convincing myself I might have heard her wrong. "Groundskeeper? Cameron?"

My thoughts spun so fast, I couldn't even form a full sentence. My mom was oblivious as she spread the little cardboard stencils out on the table. "I've been keeping a close eye on him for the past few weeks. He's proven himself to be dependable and skilled, and he's just what we need to fill Virgil's shoes."

The idea of Cameron staying here permanently while I'd been bracing myself to lose him knocked the breath right out of my lungs. I sputtered out my next words. "And–and–and what did he say? Is he going to take the job? When did you ask him?"

"A few days ago. He hasn't accepted it, and I'm not sure he will. I think he was caught off guard."

Yeah, so was I.

My pulse pounded in my ears as I busied myself with the paintbrushes, spreading them out again even though they were already perfectly lined up. I was hardly aware of my own movements.

Why hadn't he mentioned this?

If he was really considering staying, wouldn't I have been the first to know? Unless he *wasn't*. Unless he'd already made up his mind, and the answer was no. Or maybe he'd tried to tell me last night while we were dancing, but I'd silenced him before the words could come out.

A pang of regret shot through my body. If I hadn't refused to hear him out when he tried to open up, maybe I'd know where his head really was. I thought I was just protecting my heart, but all that did was push him away. And, in the process, I'd probably sent the wrong message.

I convinced myself it was just a classic case of miscommunication. Or rather, an *avoidance* of communication altogether. That was even worse.

Glancing up at the grandfather clock at the top of the stairs, I gauged how much time I had left before Cameron's son would arrive. All we needed was to have a face-to-face conversation and a chance to actually hash everything out.

If Cameron needed to tell me he was still leaving, I could cope with that. I'd already spent the entire day grappling with that reality. That ending was always inevitable, and in a way, I'd been preparing myself for it the entire month.

But if there was even the slightest chance he might stay, I wanted to find out as soon as possible. Just a simple *yes* or *no* could calm the turmoil in my heart.

"Did you hear me?"

I blinked up at my mom, realizing she'd moved closer and was now watching me expectantly. "What?"

"Delia was supposed to facilitate the pumpkin-painting this evening, but she's sick. I have to check on some things outside, and Marci... well, Marci said she dislikes children. Could you oversee everything here?"

"Yeah, I suppose. When?"

The second the words left my mouth, a family spilled into the lobby from the hallway, their two daughters darting straight for the pumpkin table. "Can we paint one?" the younger girl asked, holding one of the little orange pumpkins against her black cat dress.

My mom glanced from the kids to me with a sheepish grin. "Now?"

I almost told her I had something else I needed to take care of first, but after the conversation we'd just had, I couldn't bring myself to let her down. So I gave her a quick smile before jumping into hostess mode, handing paint smocks to the two little girls. "Who's ready to paint?"

As I opened the acrylic paint sets for the girls, my mom slipped away to take care of the pre-Halloween activities going on outside. I faked a cheerful voice and helped the girls align stencils while making small talk with their parents about Michigan weather. I did my best to play the part.

But internally, I was replaying every second of my last night with Cameron and wishing like hell I'd handled it differently. I kept forcing a smile while glancing up at that grandfather clock, wondering where Cameron was at this very minute and whether he'd made up his mind about leaving.

The revolving door creaked again, and a little boy with messy blond hair came bounding into the lobby. He seemed alone, at first, but a woman came in after him a few seconds later, dragging a little red suitcase behind her. She shook her head, grabbing him by the hand when she caught up. "I told you to wait for me, James."

My stomach dropped. Before I could fully process that this was Cameron's son, he wriggled from his mom's grasp and ran straight toward the table, pulling out a chair like this was set up just for him. "What's this for? Is that a bat? Can I paint a pumpkin? Hey! Why are some pumpkins white? Can I paint a white one?"

"Um, of course, as long as it's okay with your mom?" I looked at the woman behind him, who looked exhausted as she wrestled with his suitcase. She had a messy bun slipping loose at the nape of her neck, and an oversized sweatshirt that hung off one shoulder.

"I guess you can paint one while we wait on your dad," she said, turning to me as she let out a little laugh. Vanessa was pretty, with a round face and full lips. "I'm so sorry. He asks a lot of questions."

"It's totally fine. I just hope I have the answers," I said back, smiling as I picked up a paint smock. "Hey buddy, could you wear this so you don't get any paint on that cool dinosaur t-shirt?"

He looked down at his shirt like he'd just remembered what he was wearing. "It's a T-rex. That means 'tyrannosaurus.'"

"Wow," I said, helping him slip the smock over his head. "That is a big word for a little guy like you. What's your favorite kind of dinosaur?"

He was already reaching for one of the paint sets, only partially paying attention to me. "Um, maybe a stego... hey, I want to use this red paint! I'm going to make a red ghost and it's going to be so, so spooky."

I helped him pry open the little container of red paint, noticing his green eyes and the familiar shape of his nose and chin. He was a miniature version of Cameron, like someone had just pressed copy and paste when he was born. He painted a red ghost on his white pumpkin, sticking the tip of his tongue out while he concentrated.

I blinked hard, my throat tightening as I watched him work, jibber-jabbering to himself while his mom typed a text message behind his chair. I hadn't expected it to hit me like this, but something about being here with Cameron's son made my eyes sting. Here was this piece of his life that I'd only ever heard about in the stories he told, sitting right in front of me and looking so much like his dad it made my heart swell.

"James, your dad's on his way down here," Vanessa said, glancing up from her phone.

James gasped and thrust his brush into the container of paint like he was in a hurry. I held my breath on the other side of the table, doing my best to appear calm. Normal. And not at all like someone who was screaming on the inside.

It didn't take Cameron long to make his way down to the lobby. He emerged from the long hallway looking freshly showered, with damp hair, a clean white tee, and dark jeans–and the biggest smile I'd ever seen. The second James saw him, he dropped his paintbrush on the table, leapt from his chair, and sprinted to his dad as fast as his little feet could let him. He launched himself right into Cameron's arms. "Daddy!"

Cameron caught him effortlessly and scooped him up, holding him tight against his chest with his eyes closed. Truly soaking in the moment. "I missed you, James Bean."

The way he buried his nose in James's hair made my ovaries ache almost as much as my heart. Seeing him shirtless and sweaty didn't even come close to how attractive he was as a dad, holding James like he was the most precious thing in the world.

"James, you're getting paint on your dad's clothes." Vanessa shook her head at the red splotch on the front of Cam's shirt. It almost looked like blood, but with it being the day before Halloween, he didn't really look out of place.

"It's alright." Cameron set James down on the ground, stealing a quick glance my way. "Whatcha been painting down here, little man?"

James pulled Cameron by the hand toward the craft table to show him his messily painted pumpkin. "Look, these are ghosts. I made it for you, Daddy!"

"Wow, that's really cool." Cameron stuck his hands in his back pockets, glancing back and forth from me to Vanessa. "Uh, have you guys met my friend, Lucy?"

He nodded toward me, and I nervously wiped my palms on my dress before reaching across the table to shake Vanessa's hand. "Sorry I didn't introduce myself before," I said. "I help with operations around here."

She grinned with wide, curious eyes, and I got the sense she'd immediately clocked my relationship with Cameron. "Oh, it's nice-"

"Don't let her lie to you," Cameron said with a little chuckle. "She doesn't just 'help.' She practically runs this place."

I just let out a nervous laugh, dropping my gaze to James, who was adding black eyes and mouths to his ghosts. "And you're James, right?"

"Uh huh. James Alexander Fox."

"Wow!" I tucked my hair behind my ears, trying as hard as I could to play it cool. Was Vanessa judging me? "I heard you really like trains. Is that true?"

The kid finally looked up from his pumpkin. "Yeah. My dad's going to show me a real caboose!"

"It's all he's been talking about," Vanessa said, rolling her eyes in a playful way. "We caught a glimpse of it on the way here, and he went nuts."

"And James, guess what?" Cameron gripped his son's shoulder. "Lucy gave me a book about real trains to show you. It's upstairs. Why don't you finish up here so we can go check it out?"

The boy stood on his chair, bending over his pumpkin as he painted the last remaining details. I half-listened to Vanessa and Cameron go over the contents of James's suitcase and their pick-up arrangements for Sunday. "Well, I'm going to head out, then," she said once everything was settled. "I love you, James. Be good."

"Bye, Mommy."

Vanessa gave James a big squeeze, kissing him on the cheek before turning her attention to me. "And it was nice to meet you, Lucy."

"You too, Vanessa," I said before remembering neither she or Cameron had mentioned her name during introductions. She smiled back at me with an amused look in her eyes because we both knew I'd just told on myself.

I rinsed a used paintbrush in a cup of water, unable to shake the thought that this was the same woman who tore Cameron's heart out just a couple years ago. I'd villainized her in my head, but she was warm and friendly now, even telling Cameron "good luck and godspeed" with a laugh before she slipped out.

Cameron stood opposite the table from me, resting one hand on the back of James's chair as he added some sloppy bats to his pumpkin.

"I'm sorry if that was weird," he said quietly.

"No, it wasn't at all. I think she was figuring some things out, though," I noted, searching his eyes for some kind of reaction. He just nodded, staring down at James's masterpiece.

For a minute or two, we both just stood there and watched him paint, and I said goodbye to the other family at the end of the table, who carried their finished pumpkins toward their room. And then there was silence again.

The longer we didn't talk, the more my curiosity grew. Was there a possibility Cameron would stay? Or was this really his last weekend here? Knowing there wasn't a chance I'd get him alone before he checked out on Sunday, I inhaled, worried this might be my only opportunity.

"Cam."

His eyes flicked up to my face as he adjusted the hem of this t-shirt.

"I know about my mom's offer."

Cameron went completely still as James hummed in his seat while he painted. His chest rose with an inhale, and finally, he said, "Yeah, I wondered if she had mentioned that to you."

"She said she asked you a few days ago. Why didn't you tell me?"

He shifted his weight on his feet, lifting a hand to touch the curly hair on the back of James's head. "Because I haven't figured it out yet, and I didn't want to bring it up until I had an answer. Didn't want to give you... false hope."

I sucked in a breath. "Oh. Are you leaning toward saying no?"

"I'm not leaning toward any decision right now." Cameron stared blankly at James's pumpkin, still avoiding my gaze. "It's a huge, life-altering step to take, and I have to consider all the factors."

"Right. And... I'm sorry. I shouldn't have brought it up now." There was so much more I wanted to say, but this wasn't the time. Last night would have been the ideal time to lay all of this out, but I'd already fucked that up. Feeling stupid, I shifted my attention back to James. "Hey buddy, do you know what your ghosts need?"

"What?"

"Glitter." I reached for a shaker of black glitter and held it in front of his widening eyes. "Do you want to try it?"

"Yes!" He grabbed the container from my hand and tried to shake it, but no glitter came out. "It's not working."

"Here, let me help." I made my way around to his side of the table, and Cameron stepped out of the way so I could slide in behind James's chair. I opened the container, and with my hand over his, I showed him how to shake the glitter over the ghosts. "Look at that, see?"

"They're sparkly ghosts now!"

I laughed, letting him take over. "They're perfect."

The boy grinned up at me with big, bright eyes that reminded me *so much* of his dad's. "Are they still spooky?"

"*Very* spooky."

"Spooky and messy," Cameron said, letting out a chuckle. "Who's carrying this up to the room, kid? Me or you?"

I rubbed my palms together, shaking away some of the glitter. "If you want, you can leave it behind the front desk and pick it up on Sunday at checkout," I offered, my voice faltering on that last word.

Checkout.

There was a finality to that word that felt a little too heavy all of a sudden. I'd known for a month that Cameron would eventually check out of The Underwood Hotel for good, but saying it out loud made it feel real. And with there being the possibility he could stay, the idea of him *choosing* to leave when he didn't even have to made my throat tighten.

This didn't have to be the end, but it probably was.

"That's not a bad idea," Cameron said, scratching the back of his neck. "Hopefully that paint dries before the drive to Kalamazoo."

I swallowed that lump in my throat. "I'm afraid your truck may be covered in glitter by the end of that drive."

"Probably," he said, and I couldn't bring myself to look at him, let alone ask the question clawing at the back of my mind. Would that truck turn around after he took James home? Or was that going to be the last I'd ever see of Cameron Fox, the man who walked into this hotel a month ago and made it feel more like home to me than it ever had?

Chapter Twenty-Two

Cameron

"Boy, this town really knows how to do Halloween," I muttered to myself as I stepped over spilled popcorn in the middle of Main Street. The fog machine in front of Red Door Antiques pumped out so much smoke, I could hardly see the jack-o-lanterns in the shop windows.

Even Lucy's vivid descriptions of Halloweenfest couldn't have prepared me for the chaos downtown. The streets were lined with vendor tents, food trucks, and rickety carnival rides. James, all decked out in striped overalls and a conductor hat, was disheartened when I told him I didn't trust the shoddy construction on the Ferris wheel. But the magician performing tricks on the street corner quickly stole his attention, cutting the tantrum short.

He pulled me through throngs of people on the sidewalk so we could get a front-row view of the man dressed like a skeleton who was theatrically pulling a never-ending string of handkerchiefs from his fisted hand. James was mesmerized, clutching his hat with both hands with his mouth hanging open.

"Are you taking notes?" I looked over my shoulder to find Wesley grinning at me, Greta tucked closely by his side. Their arms were linked together, and she was holding a caramel apple.

"Hey, I thought you left town already?"

He glanced at Greta, who adjusted the cat ears she was wearing. "Well, plans changed," he said, and the two of them exchanged flirty looks. "I'm staying in Underwood for a couple more days. I didn't want to miss all this."

"Your son is adorable, Cameron," Greta said, bending down to his level. I couldn't help but notice the way Wesley beamed at her like he was already falling in love. "I love your costume! Are you a train conductor?"

"Yup! Look what I got!" He reached into the pocket of his overalls for his wooden train whistle. I let him toot it just twice so it wouldn't disrupt the magic show. Thankfully, he didn't give me any grief about it, and he shoved it back into his pocket before plopping onto the ground to watch the magician perform a card trick.

Greta opened her mouth to say something else, but something across the street stole her attention. "I just spotted an old friend," she told Wesley, giving his arm a squeeze. "I'll be right back."

Wesley watched her walk away before shaking his head at me. "That woman kept me up all night, and somehow, she's still going."

I let out a laugh, checking on James, still sitting cross-legged between us and hanging onto the magician's every word. "Well. Seems like you're having a good time."

Though he shook his head, he smiled down at his feet. "Yeah. I just hate that we waited so long to make this happen, you know? Then again, it's probably good that we didn't have time to get too attached."

I laughed again, less heartily this time. It took a few seconds for Wesley to realize what he'd said. I tried not to notice the way his face fell like he wished he could take those words back. "Right. Smart," I said, looking down as I adjusted James's little striped hat.

Wesley stuck his hands in his pockets. "Sorry, man. That came out wrong."

"Nah, don't worry about it."

"Are you and your girl not even going to try the whole long-distance thing?"

I held my breath for a few seconds. "That's just... complicated. When I come back to Michigan, my focus will be on him. I wouldn't have time for her," I said, exhaling as I nodded toward James. "But... there's this other option that came up."

"Yeah? What's that?"

I dragged one hand along the stubble on my jaw. "Her folks offered me a job here. Permanently, as groundskeeper."

"Taking that old man's job, you mean?"

"Virgil. Yeah."

"Holy shit," Wesley blurted, before glancing down at James. "Sorry. But holy cow, that's an insane offer. Good pay?"

I nodded.

"Benefits?"

I nodded again. "And room and board."

Wesley snorted. "Okay, it was nice knowin' ya."

"I didn't say I was taking it."

"Why wouldn't you?"

Around us, the crowd cheered at the magician's latest trick, and even James was politely clapping his hands. I took a second to gather my thoughts, staring at the orange and black pennant flags snapping in the breeze between two lampposts.

"It's not that simple," I said, looking Wesley in the eyes. "To go from being a one-month fling to becoming a permanent fixture in her life? Living in the same building, and working for her parents? Is that not crazy?"

Wesley considered this for a moment while studying my face closely. "Crazy? No. I think it's crazy if you get an offer like that and walk away from it."

"I'm just saying throwing myself headfirst into something is a little terrifying." I cleared my throat, adjusting my arms against my chest. "What if it doesn't work out?"

Wesley blinked. "With the hotel, or with Lucy?"

"I don't know. Both?" My mouth went dry. "She could decide I'm not what she wants, and I'm not sure I could..." I let my voice trail off. Suddenly, I was thinking about the way my whole world was turned upside down two years ago when Vanessa chose someone else. One day I was building a life with her, and the next, I was packing my things in boxes while on the phone with a divorce lawyer.

Losing Vanessa hurt. But if Lucy ever looked me in the eye one day and told me I'm not enough? That would utterly destroy me. In just one month, she had given me back a piece of myself I didn't even know was missing. Just hearing her sweet laugh or feeling her warm embrace was enough to quiet the noise in my head. Maybe it was easier to walk away now than to risk having all of that ripped out from under me later.

"Lucy is not Vanessa, man." Wesley was a little too good at reading my thoughts. "And all I know is you've been moaning about this Tennessee job ever since we found out about it. So if you don't jump on this opportunity, I'm going to drag your ass–sorry, your *butt*–back up here myself."

James tilted his head to look up at Wesley with wide eyes, and all I could do was laugh. "It's okay. He's heard worse," I told Wesley. And then, "And I don't know. I'm just weighing my–"

I couldn't finish, because my son leapt to his feet and tugged on my jeans. "Dad, I want to go down the big slide."

He pointed at the towering carnival slide at the end of the block, where kids slid down on burlap sacks and dads like me probably fractured their tailbones. I groaned, but James's pleading eyes left me no choice.

"Fine, but I better not end up in the ER over this," I teased, and he tried to yank me in the direction of the slide. "Hold on a second, buddy."

I leaned over for a half-hug from Wesley, who turned it into a hearty embrace and slapped me on the back. "This is a good-bye hug, because I'd better not see you walk up to that jobsite in a week."

I chuckled over his shoulder. "Yeah, we'll see."

Chapter Twenty-Three

Lucy

"Janine," my dad said, flinging his red cape out of the way before he slid an arm around my mother's back. "Would you look at how beautiful our daughter is?"

At the base of the double staircase, my parents stared at me with matching smiles—my dad in his vampire costume, which he wore for maybe the fifteenth year in a row, and my mom in a black turtleneck and dangly candy corn earrings.

"She really is," she agreed. "You'd think that dress was tailored just for you, sweetheart."

"Aw, you two are going to make me blush," I said, smoothing one hand over the beaded fringe on my champagne-colored, 1920s-style dress. On my collar, I'd pinned the art deco brooch I'd found at the antique store with Cameron. And Greta helped me with my hair that morning, shaping it into sculpted finger waves while gushing about her second night with Wesley. Nobody understood who I was meant to be until I explained it, but at least I could pass for a generic flapper girl.

Now, I stood in the lobby with my parents, handing out candy to a steady stream of children—some of them hotel guests, others wandering in from the festival down the street. It had been well over a decade since I participated in this little tradition of ours, and my parents were downright gleeful to have me there that night.

From the lounge, Greta's smoky voice carried over the rowdy crowd as she launched into "I Put a Spell on You." Through the front windows, I could just barely make out the lights from the Ferris wheel rising above Halloweenfest. Every time another family pushed through the revolving door, they let in a rush of cool air and a swirl of dead leaves.

I hadn't realized how much I'd missed all of this until I was back in it.

My heart skipped a beat when I spotted Cameron approaching the door just behind James, who struggled to carry a giant pumpkin plushie he must have just won. "Slow down, Bean," Cameron warned, but it was too late. James's foot caught on the revolving door, and he tumbled right into the lobby. We all gasped as his knee hit the metal strip on the threshold and the stuffed pumpkin went flying across the room. His wailing cries came before Cameron could even scoop him up.

Simultaneously, my mom and I dropped our candy bowls on the table behind us and rushed to his aid. Cameron lifted James to the reception desk and pulled up his pant leg to reveal a nasty scrape on his knee, blood already trickling down his shin. "Oh goodness! I'll get our first aid kit," my mom said in between James's loud sobs.

Cameron cradled James's head against his chest. "Hey, bud. It's going to be okay. We're going to get you all patched up and then you can show them that pumpkin we won."

I reached for the Kleenex box beside Marci, who looked like she wanted nothing to do with this situation, and pulled out three tissues. I used them to carefully wipe the blood from James's shin. "I saw that pumpkin. It went flying when you fell, didn't it?"

James sniffled, looking over my shoulder at the plushie as my dad bent over to pick it up. "It's m-mine."

"I bet you won that at Halloweenfest." I said, glancing at the first aid kit my mom pushed across the counter toward me. I flipped open the lid and tore open a package of antiseptic wipes. "This might sting, but I'm going to get you cleaned up before I put on the band-aid, okay?"

James whimpered, burying his face in his dad's flannel shirt as I took care of his wound. I could feel Cameron's eyes on me as I carefully smoothed the band-aid over James's skin, making my hands a little clumsier than usual. It struck me then that this was the first we'd seen each other all day, and the sudden nearness of him made my pulse quicken. In my peripheral vision, I caught his gaze trailing up my vintage dress and landing on the brooch at my collar. I turned my head, and our eyes met for the briefest second, but he quickly looked down at his son's knee.

"All done," I said, turning my attention back to James. My dad handed him the pumpkin plushie, and he clutched it close to his chest, looking a little overwhelmed with all these adults surrounding him now. Cameron gently tugged down the pant leg of his train conductor costume. "Does it still hurt, or does it feel a little better now that Lucy took care of you?"

"It's better," he said, rubbing his eyes. And then, the basket of skeleton keys caught his attention, each of them with their numbered keychains shining beneath the chandelier. "What are those for?"

My mom reached over and shook the basket. "We have to polish the keys every now and then so they stay shiny."

James twisted around on the counter so he could plunge one hand into the basket. "Can I do it?"

"James–" Cameron started.

But my mom said, "Sure!" just as my dad made a joke about free child labor. And before we knew it, James was cross-legged on the floor behind the reception desk, his injured knee and stuffed pumpkin forgotten as he carefully polished the keys with a white cloth my mom handed him.

Cameron leaned against the reception desk beside me, both of us giggling at the way James incorrectly read off the number on each key before he wiped it clean. "Wow. We just bobbed for apples and rode a carousel, but I think this might be the happiest he's been all day."

I laughed, my shoulder lightly brushing against his. "We may just add him to the payroll and keep him around."

His smile lingered a second, and I couldn't help noticing the way a lock of his blond hair fell across his forehead. I fought the impulse to reach up and smooth it back, knowing I probably wouldn't touch him like that again.

Cameron cleared his throat and drummed his fingers on the counter. "Hey, Mrs. Wheeler?" My mom, watching James with her hands on her hips, looked up. "Could you keep an eye on James while I talk to Lucy in private for a minute?"

Her lips parted, and her eyes bounced from my face to Cameron's like she was trying to figure us out. "Um–yes, of course," she said, blinking a few times before moving close to James. And as Cameron nodded for me to follow him down the hall, I caught my mom glancing over her shoulder at us, the corners of her lips lifting in a faint smile.

Was that... approval?

Cameron and I fell into step as we walked across the lobby toward the quiet hallway that branched off from the reception area. Greta's voice and all the noise from the Halloween festivities faded behind us.

"I wasn't sure I'd get to speak to you alone today, Lucy," Cameron said, his hand brushing the back of mine as we walked. "Or should I say... Connie."

I stopped in my tracks and turned to him, blinking in surprise. "Connie?"

"You're dressed like Connie Hathaway, aren't you?" He jerked his chin at the portrait of the original hotel owners on the wall—Edmund

Hathaway with his bowtie, and Connie with her art deco brooch and hair just like mine.

It was disarming, the way Cameron understood me so well after just a month of knowing me. "You are literally the only person who recognized it."

"I mean, this is one of the few pieces of art in this damn place I'm not terrified to look at when I walk by. Of course I recognized it."

We both laughed, and Cameron's gaze drifted to the portrait beside the Hathaways–the one of my grandparents, with their names etched in a little brass plate just below the frame.

He folded his hands behind his back. "You look more like this woman, though."

"That's my grandmother."

"That's what I thought," he said, and we took a couple more slow steps down the hall, moving toward the portrait of my parents, taken the year they took over as owners. They looked so youthful and carefree, but in a way, they'd hardly changed. We lingered in front of their portrait for a moment before drifting down to the last frame. But at the end of the row, instead of another photograph, there was an antique mirror. Staring at my reflection, I adjusted my crooked brooch and smoothed my hair before looking over at Cameron.

He was already watching me, his face completely solemn in the glass. Even in our most intimate moments, those green eyes had never stared at me with such intensity. In the mirror, I watched him reach around to his back pocket and pull out a folded, white piece of paper.

"What's that?" I asked, staring down at the note.

When he unfolded it, I recognized the handwriting immediately—*my* handwriting. It was the note I'd written him that day he helped me move tables in the rain.

Give this man whatever he wants.

♡ *Lucy*

For a few seconds, I couldn't move. I stared at my own words, unaware at first that he was trying to hand me the little paper. Finally, I accepted it, looking into his eyes. "What's this for?"

"I..." Cameron paused to take a breath. "Before I make a decision about whether I stay or go, I want to know what's in your heart. We didn't get to talk last night, so I'm asking you now: do you want me to stay here, Lucy?"

He took a step closer, placing a hand on my hip to nudge my body to the side of the hallway. The movement brought us close enough that I could feel the heat from his body as he gazed down into my eyes.

"Our month is up," he continued. "November's just a few short hours away now, and we're past the point of pretending that what we had was just something temporary we can both easily forget. But if I'm wrong about that, just tell me."

The note trembled in my hand.

Of course I wanted him to stay. God, I wanted that more than any-thing. The thought of going into November without him felt unbear-able, like the days ahead would be darker, lonelier, and colder without him. But reason and logic fought their way to the front of my mind, reminding me that this was about more than just *wanting.*

I drew in a long, shaky breath. "Cameron," I began, my voice trem-bling. Could he tell I was holding back a sob? "What's in my heart shouldn't influence your decision to accept this job offer or not. You have to make the best choice for you and James. My presence here—and my feelings about you—can't be the reason you decide to stay or go."

"I know, Lucy," he said, inching even closer. His voice was just as shaky as mine. "But I don't want to plant myself somewhere that I might not belong. This is your home, *your* family's legacy. The last thing I want is to be the reason you feel... trapped."

My brain scrambled to interpret what he was saying. "You think it would make me feel trapped?"

"I mean, I don't know." His Adam's apple bobbed, and his eyes bounced from one of mine to the other like he was reading me. "I was always meant to exit your life at the end of the month. And if my sticking around interferes with your plans, I need to know. I don't want to stay where I'm not wanted."

My eyes burned from the tears I'd been desperately trying to hold back. But after a month of holding my emotions in, I knew a flood was about to break loose. If not tears, then words. "Of course you're wanted," I blurted, letting out a sound that was something between a whimper and a laugh. I stared up at his boyish face, the one I was beginning to fall in love with and couldn't imagine losing now.

And that's when the rambling began.

"Cam." My voice cracked and I sniffled before letting the words just tumble right out. "The thought of you staying here, of us having a future, of me getting to know James better and being part of your lives excites me more than I can express. Getting to experience every season with you here at the hotel would almost feel like a fairy tale—which is why the idea of you walking away absolutely *crushes* me."

The last words came out in a broken whisper.

God, I'd just spewed my innermost feelings at him without holding back, but then again, this is what he'd asked for. The note crunched in my fisted hand as Cameron's palm slid from my hip to my lower back.

"But none of that matters," I rushed out. I would not beg him to stay. If I did, and he chose me out of pity or pressure, I'd never forgive myself. "It's about what *you* want. You should only stay if you can picture a future here, with or without me in it. You can choose this job without choosing me, and I won't stand in your way."

"Lucy," he said, letting a quiet laugh slip out. With one hand firm against my back, his other one reached up to hold my face. "Are you kidding? I want everything you said, too."

Cameron's mouth crashed into mine and I dropped the note on the floor, clutching the front of his flannel shirt. He kissed away every shred of doubt I had about whether or not he wanted me in his future. His lips pressed even harder against mine as he pulled my body flush against his.

We only pulled apart when a family in coordinating superhero costumes moved down the hallway past us. They smiled politely at us as they passed, their candy buckets practically overflowing. The two young kids were negotiating a trade deal with their Kits Kats and Starburst.

When I finally looked back at Cameron and saw the unmistakable certainty in his eyes, it fully hit me that he was choosing to stay. And he confirmed it by picking up the note, slipping it back in his pocket, and saying, "So... tell me again what it's like here at Christmastime."

It struck me then that Cameron would be spending Christmas *here*, with me. And maybe James would get to see all the decorations and twinkling lights, too.

"Well," I said, biting down on my bottom lip as I led him back down the hall. "Every year, we host a gingerbread house contest in the lobby. And of course, there's always an enormous Christmas tree between the staircases. Virgil rents a lift so he can decorate the top while my mom barks orders at him from the floor."

"Why am I not surprised?" Cameron asked with a laugh. "Do you think I'd be able to handle that?"

"That might be your true test," I teased.

We re-entered the lobby, where James was seated on the reception desk again, ringing the little bell and shouting "Happy Halloween!" at every guest who passed. My mom and dad laughed, encouraging him further, and even Marci couldn't fight back an amused grin as she watched on.

"Hey Bean," Cameron said, leaning against his elbows next to James. He reached over to silence the little brass bell. "Did you know that at Christmastime, there's always a big, big tree over there by the stairs?"

James's eyes lit up as he gazed across the lobby. "With a star on top?"

Cameron looked over his shoulder at me, and I scooted in closer. "Yes. The biggest, sparkliest gold star you'll ever see," I answered.

He looked up at his dad. "I want to see it, Daddy. Can I come see the Christmas tree?"

Cam playfully wrapped his hands around James's ankles dangling over the front of the reception desk. "You know what? I think you might. And I heard there's a gingerbread house contest, too. And someone even told me there would be sleigh rides and carolers."

He'd remembered.

My mom, never one to miss a beat, tilted her head with curiosity. "Mr. Fox, does this mean what I think it means?"

Cameron glanced over at me before giving my mom a warm half-smile. "Let me sort out a few things before I make it official. But I think this opportunity you've offered me is too good to pass up, Mrs. Wheeler."

"That's wonderful to hear." My mom turned and smiled at my dad, who slid his arm around her waist. They almost looked like that couple in their portrait down the hall, all happy and glowing. My mom's gaze shifted back to Cameron, but then she arched a brow at me. "Now is there something else I should know?"

Cameron and I exchanged quick, guilty, looks and his cheeks flushed the slightest shade of pink. That was probably enough for my mom to reach the proper conclusion about us—but with James sitting right there, that would have to be enough for right now.

"I'm just glad he's sticking around," I said, hoping that answer would satisfy her.

"Well, we're happy to welcome you to the Underwood family, son," my dad said, stepping forward to shake Cam's hand across the desk. "I know Virgil is going to insist on hanging around for a bit to show you the ropes on some things."

"Good," Cameron said with a laugh. "I may need that. Just as long as he doesn't push himself too hard."

"Virgil, push himself?" my mom joked, and the small talk continued just like Cameron was already one of us. As I watched him standing there, fitting in so seamlessly, I realized how natural this all felt.

It wasn't the welcoming glow of the chandelier, the familiar cracks in the floor tiles, or the cozy fireplace in the lounge that made this place feel like home.

It was the *people*.

The ones who built it.

The ones who carried it forward.

And the ones who were there now, proving I was always meant to find my way back at exactly the right time. And I knew, with absolute certainty, that what started in October was the beginning of forever.

Underwood Hotel Dedicates Orchard to Longtime Groundskeeper

The Underwood Hotel held a dedication ceremony Saturday morning for the Virgil E. McKinley Memorial Orchard, a new cluster of apple trees planted along the north edge of the historic property.

Virgil McKinley, who passed away last August, served as the groundskeeper for The Underwood Hotel for more than fifty years. Even after retirement, McKinley continued to volunteer at the hotel, sweeping walkways, greeting guests, and assisting with the boiler.

"He used to spend more time at this place than he did at home," his wife, Rosemarie McKinley, said. "There were many evenings I had to drag him away from here."

The newly dedicated orchard, planted with twenty apple trees, will be open to guests each fall for apple-picking and other seasonal events. Hotel staff say they hope the orchard will become "a living reminder" of the man who devoted his life to the place.

The dedication ceremony drew more than 100 people, many of whom shared personal stories of McKinley's kindness and hard work. Hotel owners Lucy and Cameron Fox stood with their children—James (14), Violet (9), and Corinne (7)—as former owner Janine Wheeler gave a speech honoring McKinley.

"Virgil never asked for recognition," Wheeler said. "But he gave more than five decades of his life to this place. Just like these apple trees will bear fruit year after year, his work continues to shape the experience of everyone who visits."

Guests were invited to walk the orchard path following the ceremony, where tables offered warm cider and maple pecan fudge from the hotel's candy store.

"Virgil taught me a lot," Cameron Fox said as the morning wrapped up. "Not just about maintaining the grounds, but about taking pride in everything we do here. He showed me that this hotel is more than just a business. We want it to feel like a home away from home for all of our guests."

The new orchard is one of several changes at The Underwood Hotel in 2035. "We would also like to invite the public to join us for the ribbon-cutting of our new library next month," Lucy Fox said, noting that the room was inspired by century-old photographs of the hotel's original interior.

The Foxes, who took ownership of the hotel two years ago, have overseen the hotel's expansion while maintaining its historic charm. "It's important to us to carry on the legacy of the hotel's past owners while also introducing new guest experiences," Fox continued. "It's a careful balance."

The orchard dedication stands as both a tribute to a longtime caretaker and a sign of The Underwood Hotel's continued growth.

Acknowledgements, etc.

I like to call this unplanned book my "little DIY project" because I did a lot of the "extra" stuff on my own due to time constraints. While it had me cursing at my laptop screen some nights, I'm really proud of the way everything came together. (I didn't have "relearn Photoshop" on my bingo card for 2025!)

But just because I worked on it alone doesn't mean I was *really* alone in this. I'm so grateful for close friends, family, and dedicated readers (particularly my Patreon subscribers) who weighed in on important details and reminded me why I love writing in the first place. Your support and enthusiasm carried me through the entire process! I would specifically like to acknowledge Brooke, Em, Taylor, Haley, Taneil, Marci, Krista, Corinna, Elizabeth, Ali, and Katie (the Woodvale Smut Sluts & VIP members) who continuously invest in me and my stories.

And let's not forget the authors on Threads coming to my rescue any time I was stuck. Whether it was advice, encouragement, or your unhinged millennial GIFs (seriously, are we the only generation that can communicate better with a Jim Halpert GIF than words??) you kept me sane while I finished this book.

Thank you to all the librarians, booksellers, and bookish influencers who support indie authors.

And to Holden: I'm sorry I keep giving random background characters your name. But I probably won't stop.

9 798218 815417